O9-AJO-623

A PERFECT CHRISTMAS GIFT

LORI WILDE

DEC 2021

CHAPTER 1

EVAN CONNER OPENED the front door and frowned at the elf standing on the porch.

This elf was a petite redhead wearing a full-fledged red and green costume fitted with a pointed hat, pointed-toe shoes, and jingle bells. Lots and lots of jingle bells. A sprinkle of freckles crossed her pert nose; a wide grin plucked up the corners of her mouth, and her deep green eyes sparkled like diamonds.

Yes, sir, a really, really cute elf.

But what was she doing here? Puzzled, he peered over her shoulder to see if Santa and a few reindeer might be lurking around, but no, she was alone.

"May I help you?" he asked, bracing for the answer. Nothing about this weird business trip was turning out the way he'd expected.

"Hi! I'm Dr. Chloe Anderson, the vet," the elf said. She extended her hand to the jangle of the jingle bell bracelet at her wrist. "You called about a dog?"

Evan introduced himself and shook her hand, relieved to know who she was but still perplexed by her wardrobe choice. "Thanks for coming. Um, nice outfit..."

She laughed. "Sorry about the elf costume. It's photos with Santa day at my veterinarian clinic, and I didn't have time to change. Our pet parents love to have some holiday fun, so we all dress up and pose with the dogs and cats for Christmas pics."

Evan grinned. Chloe Anderson chattered a mile a minute. The whole time she was talking, her hands moved, and her eyes danced, and her smile lit her face. "Sounds like a great way to turn a tidy little profit."

Her smile vanished, and she frowned at him like a disappointed fifth-grade teacher.

"Excuse me, but we don't make a profit from the photos. We charge nothing to the pet parents."

"Why not?" he asked, fascinated.

"We do it in the spirit of Christmas. You've heard of that, haven't you?" Her voice turned a tad tart on that last part.

He held up both palms. "I didn't mean to offend."

"It's okay." Her smile was back. "But I can tell you're not from Kringle."

What did that mean? Feeling slightly offended, Evan pushed the front door open. "C'mon in."

She jingled over the threshold, and he couldn't suppress his smile. She sounded like a one-woman parade.

"I am sorry about my comment," he apologized again. "I'm a corporate lawyer, and if you don't mind a little friendly business advice, a small vet practice such as yours should maximize all opportunities for a profit. You could make quite a lot off those pet photographs if you have a big turnout."

The look Chloe gave him could melt paint off a car. "I could never do that. I do suggest that our pet parents donate to the local animal shelter, but I would *never* try to profit from it."

Her attitude toward profit made him want to shake his head, but as she continued staring at him, he realized what she did or didn't do wasn't his concern. He was only in Kringle, Texas, for two weeks, and then it was back to his life in Dallas.

"Whatever works for you." He shut the door.

She looked a little embarrassed that she'd overreacted. "That's okay. I shouldn't have gotten so upset. I just don't want you to think that I'm all about money."

Many retorts occurred to Evan, but he kept his

mouth shut. Instead, he nodded, which she must have taken as agreement.

"Mind if I leave a few things here while I look at the dog?" She moved into the large foyer and stopped at a side table. "I don't want to scare her with all the jingling."

"Of course," he said, curious what exactly she intended.

She set down the small medical bag, took off her hat, and slid the felt elf covers off her shoes. She also took off armbands festooned with jingle bells. When she finished, she still looked like an elf, just less noisy.

Chloe glanced around. "I didn't know someone rented the Madison place. Last I heard, Kitty and Dwayne were still living in Dallas. It's a nice... um...house."

Evan didn't blame her for hesitating. The word "house" hardly described the place. 'Sprawling mansion" was the phrase that came to mind, and the estate fit into the small town of Kringle like a giant wart on a puppy's face.

"My boss rented it," he said, not wanting her to think he wasted money on lavish housing.

When his boss, Peter Thomas, had brought up this trip and "volun-told" Evan he was coming, too, Peter said his goal was to make amends to his home-town. A heart attack last month had Peter reconsidering his life as a corporate lawyer, and now he wanted to show the people he'd hurt in the past that he'd changed.

"It's a *Christmas Carol* without the ghosts," he'd told Evan.

But so far, Peter acted more like the original Scrooge than the reformed version. For instance, renting the biggest, most ostentatious house in town was hardly the right way to show the townsfolk he wasn't greedy.

"Ready?" Chloe asked.

"This way." Evan led her to the home office. "When I got up this morning, I heard some yipping and whimpering and discovered this..."

He shoved open the French doors so that Chloe could see the small light-brown dog in the room's corner. The dog had made herself a little bed out of what had once been a fine oriental rug and two expensive throw pillows. Inside the makeshift bed lay the dog and three small puppies.

"She must have come in through the doggie door. Whoever is in charge of this house should have secured it."

"True." Chloe approached the dog and knelt in front of her.

The little dog thumped her tail against the floor and looked up at the vet with moony eyes.

"Look at you, Vixen, you went and had babies," Chloe cooed.

"Vixen? You know this dog?"

Chloe nodded. "She belonged to a wonderful woman who used to live in Kringle, Vivian Kuhlmeier. Vivian passed away a few months ago at the ripe old age of ninety-seven. Everyone in town looks after Vixen. But then she vanished. We thought she'd left the area, but I'm glad to see she's okay. Better than okay. She's a mama now."

Evan stayed by the doorway while Chloe examined Vixen and her puppies. He was in over his head. Animals just weren't his thing. He hadn't grown up around them, and his parents drummed it into his head that pets were a waste of money.

When he'd told Peter about the dog, his boss had said, "Eeew, just get them out of the house."

As usual, his employer expected him to do all the dirty work. When he'd agreed to come along on this trip with Peter, he'd thought his boss would say "hi" to a few old friends, apologize for his misdeeds, and then they'd head back to Dallas.

From what he'd seen so far, Kringle was a cute town, but a small one. It shouldn't take too long for Peter to accomplish his mission, and Evan felt a bit impatient that his boss had already strung things out for three days.

He hadn't planned on spending a lot of time in this one-pony town. Even though not much happened in the corporate world during the month of December, he still wouldn't mind getting back to the office. There was always work that needed doing.

Chloe clicked her tongue. "I told Vivian repeatedly that she should get Vixen spayed, but she wouldn't do it. She had some misguided notion that spaying messed with a dog's temperament."

"Too bad you can't wave a magic wand and make people do what you want," Evan mumbled, thinking of Peter.

"I wouldn't want to be the one wielding the magic wand." Chloe sank her hands on her slim hips.

"Why not?"

"As nice as it might seem to control the world, I do believe in free will. You've got to let people be who they are, no matter how inconvenient it might be for you."

"That's a philosophical attitude."

"I find life works better when I don't impose my values onto others. But..." Chloe sighed. "Now not only does Vixen need a new home, but so do her puppies. Thankfully, at least the birth seems to have gone smoothly."

"I'm glad for that." And Evan was beyond glad to shift the new mother out of the house. Dealing with his boss was difficult enough. He knew nothing about taking care of animals, especially a litter of puppies. "So, you'll take her with you?"

"No, she should stay here."

Evan was so certain she was going to say yes that it took a minute for her answer to sink in. He was already planning how he was going to move the dog into the vet's car.

He blinked. "Stay h-here?"

"Vixen and the puppies will be fine," she said, as if the animals' health was his top concern. "Just keep the room warm and make sure she has food and water. She needs bonding time with her puppies."

"W-What?" he asked, hoping he'd heard wrong, and he felt like a dolt. "She has to stay here? Are you sure?"

He looked at the little dog. Sure, she was cute with her big brown eyes and her little black nose, but she worried him. What if something went wrong?

Chloe had been patting the dog, but now she turned to look at him. "Yes. She should stay here for a few more days. There's no reason to move her."

Evan frowned. Vixen looked content with her puppies snuggled next to her. What the vet said made sense, but the new mom and her puppies intimidated him. He'd faced tough juries that didn't unsettle him as much as one little mama dog and her puppies.

"Um..." He glanced at Chloe, not at all happy with how this was turning out. "I guess I can handle it."

She laughed. "It's not as hard as it seems. The doggie door is right behind her, so she can go outside when she needs to. I'll help you set up food and water."

Knowing this was the best he could hope for at the moment, Evan resigned himself to his fate. "Okay."

She stood up, dusted her palms together, then came closer to him and smiled widely. The woman could be a professional smiler, she was so good at it. "Don't worry. It'll be fine. I can stop by every day after work and check on her if you'd like."

Yes, yes, he'd like, he'd like.

"Please do," he said, hating that he sounded like a drowning man begging for a life preserver but sure he needed help. "Naturally, I'll pay you for your time."

"You need not pay me each time I stop by."

Now they were on his turf—negotiations. "You've got to value your time, Dr. Anderson. People take advantage of you if you don't."

She settled her hands on her hips and smiled again. A serial smiler. He had to admit it was a darn cute smile. When Chloe smiled, it reached all the way to her eyes. And right now, her eyes twinkled like the Christmas lights strung up from every building in town. He amused her, Evan realized, like some novelty toy.

"Fine," she said. "If that's the way you want it. I'll charge you an arm and a leg each time I stop by. It's my goal to please people. I'd love to collect lots and lots of money from you. Will that make you happy?"

He couldn't help it. Evan laughed. He liked Dr. Chloe Anderson, DVM. "Yes. That will make me happy. I love being overcharged."

"Good. Then my work here is done." She bent for one last check on the dog and her puppies, then nodded to herself and straightened. "If you encounter any problems, just call me."

"Call you about what?"

Simultaneously, they turned to see Peter standing in the doorway of the home office.

Before Evan could introduce him, Chloe glared.

"Peter Thomas?" she said, her tone as chilly as an iceberg. "What are *you* doing here?"

"Hello, Chloe." Peter's voice was just as stiff as hers.

Evan glanced at his boss and then back at the diminutive vet. "I gather you two know each other?"

"Yes," they said in unison and glowered at each other.

"How is your mother?" Peter asked.

"Mom is fine, thanks." She clenched her jaw so tightly that Evan could see the muscles working underneath her skin. "How have you been?"

"Fine." Peter tipped his head and studied her outfit with a sidelong glance down the end of his nose. "Nice elf clothes."

Evan stifled a groan. His boss had insisted on apologizing to the town's residents, and he had no idea what Peter had done to alienate the vet, but he shouldn't miss this opportunity to apologize.

"That's right. Scoff at Christmas. You're oh so good at it." Chloe's killer smile was MIA.

"Peter, you came to this town for a reason. Wouldn't now be a great time to start?" Evan asked.

One eyebrow shot up on Chloe's forehead. "What reason is that?"

Peter shrugged and seemed reluctant to do what he had insisted last week needed doing. "I'm trying to make up for a few things in my past. Like Scrooge, you know, after the ghosts."

"Scrooge?" Chloe looked confused.

"Yep." Peter flashed her one of his patented lawyer smiles, big but lacking in sincerity. "I had a heart attack last month."

"Oh no," Chloe said, genuine concern in her voice. She might not like the man, but she could still empathize with him. The vet was a class act. "I'm so sorry to hear about that."

Peter waved off her concern. "It was mild, but it got me to thinking. I needed to come back to Kringle and mend a few broken fences."

"They are a little more than just broken fences, don't you think?" Chloe asked, her mouth pulled into a dubious expression.

"I know, I know a few folks in Kringle aren't big fans of mine," Peter said. "Just wanted to pop by and say 'sorry.'"

"A few?" Chloe frowned. "Peter, you convinced Kringle's primary employer to pull out of the town."

Peter shrugged. "It was a good move for my client."

"It *devastated* our local economy and left many families struggling to make ends meet. Dozens of people had to move away to find new jobs. A few folks even lost their homes. All because of *you*."

While Chloe was speaking, Peter kept bobbing his head. Evan wanted to tell him to stop it, but he knew better. Peter had a temper, which wouldn't help the present situation; however, what his boss was doing was rude.

Based on what Evan had seen so far tonight, this apology mission in Kringle was looking more and more like a disaster.

"I'm sure Peter feels terrible about what happened," Evan soothed, trying to scoot Chloe toward the door.

The last thing he wanted to do was alienate the vet. He'd almost gotten her out of the study when a small mewing noise came from Vixen and her puppies.

Peter moved around Evan and saw the dogs. "What are those mutts doing here? I hate dogs. Evan, get rid of them. Toss them outside."

Evan opened his mouth to tell his boss that he would not hurt the dogs, but before he could say anything, Chloe got in Peter's face.

"No one will harm those animals." She shook her finger at him. "Do you hear me? I will have you arrested for animal cruelty."

Evan would give her this—a regular person might find it difficult to look frightening while wearing an elf costume, but Chloe Anderson managed it.

"Keep your pants on. Fine. Sheesh. The dogs can stay." Peter headed for the door.

A little of the fire simmered down in her eyes. But Chloe did not like his boss.

"Evan, they are your responsibility. I don't want to hear or see them." Then, without another word, Pete walked out, leaving Evan and Chloe staring at each other.

Evan recovered first. "Nothing will happen to Vixen and her babies. I promise."

Chloe pulled one corner of her bottom lip up between her top teeth, and slowly, she shook her head. "I know you mean that, but I am worried about them now. I wouldn't have suggested they stay here if I'd known you were with Peter."

She had a look on her face like she'd just eaten something rotten. He would have to talk to Peter about his attitude and the way he'd treated Chloe.

Ever since his heart attack, all Peter talked about was making amends to the people he'd harmed over the years, but at this rate, he was adding people to the "make amends" pile rather than subtracting from it.

"Nothing will happen to the dogs," Evan reassured her. "I'll make sure they get good care. Peter didn't mean what he said. He's just not an animal person."

Chloe squared her shoulders like a fierce warrior going into battle and held his gaze. "You *promise* they won't be neglected?"

Evan couldn't look away from her intense gaze.

Attraction crackled between them for a few seconds as they stared at each other.

He crossed his heart. "I promise. You have my word that no harm will come to Vixen and her puppies. Please, show me what to do, and I will take good care of them."

She inclined her head. She looked from him to Vixen and her puppies and then back again, torn.

He couldn't really blame her for not trusting him. She didn't know him, and what she knew about Peter apparently wasn't good. Was she mentally lumping the two of them into the same category? Evan worked for Peter, and therefore she couldn't trust Evan either?

Hoping to convince her, he flashed his most sincere smile. "I really do promise."

"I suppose I shouldn't judge someone on the company they keep." She studied him for a long moment, and he must have passed muster because she said, "Come on, I'll help you set up the food and water."

They worked in silence for a few minutes, getting bowls from the kitchen and putting out dog food she retrieved from her vehicle.

When they finished, she sent him a solemn look. "I'm counting on you, Evan Conner, to do the right thing."

Evan didn't hesitate. "Vixen and company will be fine. I'll protect them with my life."

Finally, she smiled again, and he knew she believed him.

Weird how his stomach started tingling and he felt an airy sensation in his heart. Why did her belief in him matter so much?

"Okay," she said. "But if you don't mind a little friendly business advice, if I were you, I'd find a new boss."

Yeah, well, that thought crossed his mind once or twice today. Especially since he'd been "volun-told" to come on this trip, he'd developed uneasy feelings. The more he got to know about his boss, the less he liked him. Peter wasn't the easygoing, jovial guy he made himself out to be in the office.

As Evan walked Chloe to her SUV parked in the driveway, something else occurred to him. He'd really enjoyed getting to know Chloe, and he'd like to learn more about her.

She opened her car door. "Good luck. I'll come around before work tomorrow to check on Vixen and the babies."

"May I ask you something?"

She looked cautious, but finally said, "All right."

"Could I take you to dinner?"

Her eyes rounded, and her mouth formed a surprised little O. "Tonight?"

He nodded. "Yes. Please? I'd love to take you to dinner for helping me out with this, and I'm feeling a little lonely in this town with only Peter as company."

"I can see how isolating that must feel."

"So you'll go out to dinner with me?"

"I'm dressed as an elf." She laughed.

Now it was his turn to chuckle. "I'm fine with it, although I feel underdressed. Maybe I could find a Santa hat?"

Her eyes sparkled. "Sure, okay. Why not?"

"Really?" He'd braced for her to turn him down.

"But I have to swing by my mom's house first. In fact, I can change there, and you can meet Mom." She gave him the address. "But fair warning, if you tell her your connection to Peter, expect a little blow-back. Jilting someone at the altar doesn't tend to endear you to a person who got jilted."

"Peter dumped your mother at the altar?" Evan knew that Peter had been engaged to someone in Kringle and broken it off with no explanation, but he didn't know he'd left the bride standing at the altar. That was a jerk move.

Evan barely resisted the impulse to apologize to

Chloe, even though none of this was his fault. Still, he felt bad that his boss had hurt these people, and he was going to try his best to make sure Peter really made amends.

"I'd like very much to meet your mother," he told Chloe.

She opened her door to her silver SUV. Kringle Animal Clinic was printed on the side, along with pictures of dogs and cats. The vehicle was every bit as cute as its owner.

"Just so you know, Peter really hurt her, "Chloe said. "He shouldn't expect her simply to forgive him."

"Fair enough. He still needs to apologize. It's up to her to decide how she feels after that."

Chloe gave a quick nod and climbed in the car. "Okay. We'll see how it goes."

Evan forced a smile and then said, "I'm sure it will go great. I have a really good feeling about this."

After she pulled out of the driveway and drove off, Evan headed back inside. His assurances to the vet had been a total fib. He wished that he had a good feeling about Peter's mission in Kringle, but he didn't.

Quite the opposite.

CHAPTER 2

PETER THOMAS WAS BACK in Kringle.

Bad news all around, Chloe thought as she drove to her mom's house.

Well, except that he'd brought Evan Conner with him. Then again, Peter always *had* known how to surround himself with good people to balance out his wily ways.

Okay, she was happy to meet Evan. He seemed like a really friendly person, and it didn't hurt that he was good-looking. Tall, with deep-chestnut hair and light-brown eyes, he was definitely heartthrob material. She was attracted to him, and not just because of his looks.

Evan Conner struck her as a nice man, and her instincts about people were rarely wrong.

Still, Evan being an agreeable person didn't help with her fundamental problem.

People in Kringle did not like Peter. He'd hurt many folks, her mother one of them, when he'd left Mom standing at the altar.

Five years ago, when he'd first come back to his hometown, Chloe had been away at college, so she'd only met him once or twice. She hadn't directly witnessed the destruction—but she'd seen the aftermath. The man was trouble.

It didn't take long to arrive at her mother's one-story red brick house near the center of town. Like most houses in Kringle, she'd decorated it to the hilt for Christmas. Each tree and bush in the front yard festooned with twinkle lights.

On the lawn, her mother had placed a lighted display of three reindeer, and up by the front door was a blowup oversized snowman with a black hat and a red bow tie. Mom was a big fan of the holiday, which is why she'd retired here ten years ago after Chloe's dad passed away.

Not that Chloe could blame her mom. Kringle was a great town. It was a fun place year-round, but especially so around the holidays. But five years ago, Peter had convinced the principal employer, Kringle Kandy, to move to Dallas.

That move devastated the local economy, and even now, half a decade later, it hadn't really recovered.

Worse was the way Peter had treated her mother. He'd wined and wooed her and proposed after only a few months. But he'd left town shortly after the deal with Kringle Kandy was complete, deserting both the town and her mother.

This afternoon, he also hadn't done a thing to impress Chloe that he'd changed. She still couldn't believe what he'd said about Vixen. What evil man would threaten a sweet dog? He definitely fit the Scrooge image—the before ghosts version. She was unconvinced that he was sincere enough to grow beyond that. She couldn't help getting the feeling that his contrite act was just that—an act.

How did she break the news to her mother that Peter was back?

She parked in her mom's drive and walked to the front door. The moment her mother saw her in her costume, she burst out laughing.

"Cute," Chloe said, moving past her mother and into the house.

"Yes, sweetie, you are cute. I love the outfit."

Chloe twirled like a runway model in the living room, showing off the outfit. "Now I'm going to change."

She changed into a pair of jeans and a teal T-shirt she kept stashed in her vehicle. As a vet, she never knew when she might need a fresh change of clothes. She stared at herself in the white bathroom vanity mirror. "Might as well bite the bullet and tell her about Peter now."

Squaring her shoulders, Chloe went to break the

news, but her mom was on her cell phone. One look at her mother's expression told her someone had already beaten her to the punch.

The Kringle grapevine worked overtime.

Her mother switched off her phone and turned to Chloe. "Peter's back in Kringle."

"I know. I was just about to tell you."

"Where did you hear?"

"I stopped by the Madison place. I got a call from Pete's assistant, Evan Conner, that a stray dog had gotten into the house and had puppies. It turned out to be Vixen." For a few minutes, she caught her mom up on Vixen's progress. "So how do you feel about Peter being back in town?"

"From what Jolie Stuart said..." Her mother waved at the phone she had set on the coffee table. "He's back to make amends for all the problems he caused."

"What do you think about that?"

"It's a good thing. He *should* apologize to the folks of Kringle. He caused a lot of heartache."

"True."

Her mother shrugged and picked up an ornament from the array laid out on the coffee table and crossed the room to hang a large red ball on the front of the tree she was decorating. Canting her head, she considered the ball, and then moved it to the side. Her mother seemed perfectly calm, not at all bothered that Peter had returned.

But Chloe wasn't calm. She was worried. From the first time she'd met him, she'd gotten the feeling he was constantly on the lookout for an opportunity, a way to advance himself regardless of the impact to others.

Ruby pursed her lips and moved the ornament again.

Chloe would have offered to help with the tree, but her mother had a specific way she liked to decorate. She figured she was better off just watching since she was more of a hang-it-anywhere sort.

She plunked on the blue-flowered sofa and patted her mother's yellow cat, Belle. As always, the second Chloe sat, Belle climbed into her lap and demanded attention. Once Chloe had established a patting pace that worked for Belle, she looked at her mom, who was still hanging ornaments with a critical eye.

Petite with the same red hair as Chloe, her mother looked much younger than her fifty-nine years. She had a bright smile and a big laugh, and Chloe thought she was the most amazing mom in the world.

"Okay, Mom, now tell me the truth. How do you really feel about Peter being here? He let you down more than anyone."

Her mother had been fiddling with a snowflake ornament, but now she looked at her daughter. "It's fine," she said.

"Are you sure?"

"I know I should be heartbroken, but I'm not. That tells you that it's for the best we didn't get married. What we had wasn't genuine love. He didn't break my heart. If it had been genuine love, I would feel something now that he's come back, but I honestly don't."

"Really?"

"Life has turned out exactly the way it should have." She gave Chloe a calm smile.

Although Chloe was glad to hear her mother felt this way, in some ways, it made her sad. If her mother was right, how did you know when you'd found genuine love, the type that *would* break your heart if it didn't work out?

If genuine love meant that your heart could get broken, was love worth the risk?

Personally, she'd never gotten even close to true love. She'd dated over the years and even had a few serious relationships, but they'd ended rather unspectacularly. She hadn't been heartbroken, and neither had the guy.

Almost as if she had sensed her daughter's thoughts, Ruby said, "You'll understand one day when you truly fall in love. I was truly in love with your father. Losing him broke my heart. Losing Peter didn't."

The doorbell rang. For the holidays, her mother had set the ringtone to "We Wish You a Merry

Christmas." Kringle really was the perfect place for Ruby to live. The town was custom made for a Christmas fanatic like her.

Since she was closest, Chloe answered the door.

Both Evan Conner and Peter Thomas stood on the porch.

She gave Evan a questioning look.

"When I told Peter we were meeting at your mother's house, and we were going out to dinner, he asked to come along. I hope you don't mind."

Chloe minded him being here. She wasn't sure her mother was ready to see him, even if he hadn't broken her heart. Good manners forced her to open the door widely and say, "Welcome."

Peter walked into the house first, followed by Evan.

Chloe watched as surprise crossed her mother's face, but then she was relieved when her mother seemed unconcerned that her ex-fiancé had just walked in.

"Hello, Peter." Her mother gave him a warm smile, walked over, and gave him a quick hug. "It's nice to see you."

Peter looked at her mother with so much regret it almost made Chloe feel sorry for him.

Maybe she'd misjudged him. It looked like he had sincerely missed her mother.

"It's wonderful to see you," Peter said.

"You too." Mom quickly stepped from his embrace.

No missing it, Peter looked disappointed.

Chloe introduced Evan to her mother.

Belle rubbed against his legs, leaving an impressive band of yellow fur on his dark-blue pants. If the fur transfer bothered him, Evan didn't show it. Other than a quick glance down at Belle, his focus remained on her mother.

He shook her hand. "It's nice to meet you, Ruby. Chloe has your beautiful smile."

"Thank you, Evan. That's sweet of you to say." Ruby smiled and sent Chloe a knowing look that said, *handsome*.

Uh-oh, Chloe knew that look. Mom was cooking up matchmaking scenarios. Chloe needed to nip that in the bud.

"So, Peter, what brings you back to Kringle?" Her mother's smile was warm, but her tone held just a hint of a chill.

"I had a heart attack two months ago," Peter said. "It made me rethink a few things."

"Things?" Her mother slanted her head and studied him with a flinty glint in her eyes.

Peter shifted his weight and cleared his throat. 'Mistakes I've made. Things I regret."

"Things like single-handedly destroying Kringle's economy?" Chloe prompted. She didn't mean to be pushy, but this man owed the town a lot more than convenient apologies.

If he noticed her tone, he didn't react. Instead, he looked at her mother and said, "I decided two things after my heart attack. One, I needed to apologize to the folks of Kringle. And two, I want to have a perfect Christmas, the kind of perfect Christmas you can only have in Kringle."

Chloe wanted to jump in and say a few things to Peter, but the forgiving look on her mother's face told her to let it go. Her mother was the most loving person Chloe knew, and if she was willing to let things go, then Chloe needed to let them go too.

"I'm very sorry if I hurt you," Peter told her mother.

Ruby rewarded him with a tender smile. "Thank you for the apology. I appreciate it."

Chloe knew her mother well enough to know his apology was all her mother needed to forgive him. Heck, she'd already forgiven him years ago, even without an apology. Chloe felt as if him saying he was sorry was for his benefit rather than her mother's, and it did nothing to make Chloe believe his sincerity.

Her mother turned to Evan. "Are you here for a perfect Kringle Christmas as well?"

Evan chuckled and Chloe felt a strange little tingle in her stomach at the sound.

"Yes and no," he said. "Sure, I'd love a great

Christmas, but I work for Peter. He had me come along to make sure everything runs smoothly. It hasn't been that long since his heart attack."

"Well, Chloe and I will do everything we can to ensure both of you have a perfect Christmas. Kringle is almost magical this time of year. I'm sure you'll have a wonderful time." Her mother shot her a meaningful look. "Chloe can help make sure you have a terrific Christmas, Evan. You should spend time with her. Kringle has so many outstanding events for the holiday."

Chloe frowned at her mother's matchmaking attempts, but if he noticed it, Evan didn't comment.

"Have you seen the town?" her mother asked.

"Not really. We drove straight to the house when we got here yesterday evening. I noticed that Main Street is festive with decorations, but I haven't seen the rest of the town."

"Main Street *is* the town," Peter said. "The one street. It's a handful of businesses and then, at the end of the street, the town hall. You've had the complete tour."

Peter's tone made it clear he didn't think Kringle was much to see, but Evan simply said, "I'm looking forward to exploring, and I'm glad I'm on the trip."

Chloe imagined there was more to the story than Evan was sharing, but she didn't pry. As far as she could tell, Peter should be thankful Evan had come along. Evan helped even out Peter's tarnished image.

"Evan will also arrange the party," Peter said. "It's one of the chief things I want to happen while I'm here."

Chloe looked at Evan, who shrugged. "Peter wants to have a big Christmas Eve bash at the house."

"The Madison place is large enough to hold most of the town," Ruby pointed out. "Have you spoken to Kitty and Dwayne Madison recently? I heard they were thinking about moving back to Kringle after they retire."

"I talked to them when I rented their house for two weeks. They seemed fine," Peter said, but something in his voice made Chloe suspicious. Kitty and Dwayne had been the owners of Kringle Kandy.

"The party will amaze," Peter said. "I'll invite everyone in town."

It didn't surprise Chloe that her mother nodded. Ruby loved parties, and a Christmas Eve party would be too wonderful for her to resist.

It was getting late. Chloe headed toward the front door. "Evan and I planned to go to dinner. Peter, I guess you're coming as well, right? Mom, why don't you join us?"

She'd assumed her mother would agree, but Ruby said, "No, I think I'll stay here. I want to work on the tree."

"I'll stay and help," Peter said immediately. "I'm not hungry."

He sat next to her mother, his expression a little too self-satisfied for Chloe's comfort. Chloe looked at her mother to see if Peter staying was okay with her, but she seemed unconcerned. In fact, she'd already handed Peter a string of tangled lights to straighten.

Chloe considered also staying behind.

"Okay. Well, be sure and let us know if you want us to bring anything back," Evan said, opening the front door.

Torn, she hesitated. Wanting to go with Evan but thinking she should stay to make sure her mother would be okay.

Ruby sent her a pointed look. "Go."

"You're sure?"

Belle was still eeling between Evan's legs.

Chloe picked up Belle and held her up so Evan could see her face. "I think someone will be broken-hearted to see you leave."

Evan scratched the cat behind her ear. "I'm getting to meet many animals today."

Chloe sat Belle down and moved outside, closing the door securely behind them. "Lots of people in town have dogs or cats or both. I know it might seem that my practice would be small, but it's actually very busy. We have lots of pet lovers in Kringle."

Evan Conner drove an expensive black SUV. Everything about him screamed success. She'd bet those dress pants that Belle had covered with fur cost more than her weekly grocery bill.

He opened the passenger door for her, and she climbed inside.

"I was going to comment on the lack of animal fur in your car, but it won't be fur free for long." She nodded at his pants.

He glanced at the bands of fur Belle had left behind and smiled, which made Chloe like him even more. He'd already explained he wasn't used to pets, yet so far today he'd taken on the responsibility for a new mother and her pups and gotten coated in fur by an attention-loving cat.

"It's just fur. It will come off the car and my pants," he said. "Life comes with messes."

With that, he closed her door and headed over to his side of the car.

Chloe watched him circle the car. She better watch herself around Evan Conner. He was irresistible.

CHAPTER 3

EVAN STUDIED the menu and wondered what everything meant. Normally, he was pretty quick to catch on to things, but the meal selections at the Kringle Kafe had him baffled. What exactly was a HoHoHo burger?

"I have no clue what to order," he admitted to Chloe. "A HoHoHo sandwich?"

She laughed, the sound soft and appealing. "It's a little confusing until you get used to the Kringle lingo." She leaned over and pointed at his menu. "The names are on the front of the menu, but the descriptions are on the back. A HoHoHo is number three on the menu. Turn it over and read the description on the back."

Why in the blue blazes would anyone design a menu that was this complicated?

Evan turned the menu over and read the description. *HoHoHo, the joke is on you if you were looking for beef. It's a mushroom veggie burger.*

Chloe grinned at him over her menu. "The HoHoHo is my fav."

"Um, I guess I'll get that," he said.

"You don't have to. I get it because I'm a vegetarian. You can order whatever you like."

As someone who didn't really care one way or the other what he ate, he figured he'd just follow her lead. Agreeing was simpler, and he liked things simple. Complicated was stressful, and life was complicated enough without stressing about food.

A pert waitress named Sandy bopped over to take their order. "Excellent choice," she said, revealing red and green braces. "The HoHoHo is our number two best seller after the Kris Kringle."

Evan looked at the description of the Kris Kringle. It was a double meat chili cheese burger. His mouth watered, but he took the high road and stayed with the HoHoHo.

"So tell me about yourself," he said to Chloe, once the waitress had gone. It surprised him how much he wanted to know her better.

"Not much to tell. Born in Fort Worth. Grew up there happy. Went to A&M and was happy. Worked for a big vet clinic in Tyler for two years but was not happy. So I came here to Kringle when Mom moved. I've had my clinic for three years, and it's going great!" She flashed a smile. "Happy again."

Her version of her life made him smile as well. In an era when everyone shared everything online in minute detail, she'd condensed her entire life into a few brief sentences.

"Succinct," he said.

She shrugged, a casual little drop of her shoulders. "There's not much to tell. My life is pretty straightforward. I've been very lucky. I know that."

Truthfully, he'd met no one whose life was this straightforward. Everyone encountered bumps in the road. He had, and he'd be willing to bet that Chloe had as well. Still, it was good that she saw her life in terms of happiness and that she was happy. When he considered his life from that perspective, he wasn't as lucky.

He just couldn't put his finger on why not. He had a magnificent job. Thomas & Associates was one of the most successful corporate law practices in Dallas, and there was no doubt he was on track to make partner in the next few years.

So why wasn't he happy?

"What about you?" Chloe said. "Who is Evan Conner beneath that buttoned down appearance?"

He was about to give her a synopsis of his career when their waitress, Sandy, reappeared with their order.

Sandy set down their plates in front of them, then stepped back, rested her hands on her hips, and gave Evan a frown. "I heard you're here with Peter Thomas."

Evan hadn't been paying as much attention as he should have. He glanced up and realized Chloe, the waitress, and most of the café patrons stared at him.

"Yes. Peter is my boss."

"I'm Sandy Hughes," she said, sounding indignant, and touched her name badge. "Peter really did a number on Kringle when he convinced the Madisons to move their candy company to Dallas."

Evan knew his boss had a tendency to plow over people to get what he wanted, but he valued loyalty, and he would not badmouth Peter in front of these townsfolk. "The Madisons made their decision of their own free will. You can't blame him for recommending a move that was in their best interest."

"Best interest, my fanny." Anger flared in Sandy's eyes. "Kitty and Dwayne are in their seventies. Peter badgered and harangued them until they agreed, and now they're miserable and so are we."

"How do you know that?" Evan asked calmly. "Were you in the meetings?"

"I heard—"

"Hearsay isn't a fact."

"Spoken like a lawyer." Sandy glowered. "What's Peter got up his sleeve this time? Closing the Kringle Kafe?"

"He's not planning anything except to apologize for his actions five years ago. He will also have a party on Christmas Eve, and he's invited everyone in town. You included, Sandy."

He looked around the room at the proliferation of John Deere caps, down coats, and work boots—even on the women. Most of these people were farmers.

"*Everyone* is invited. Peter wants to make up for what happened. He's a changed man."

"Sure he is." One farmer snorted. "About as sorry as my pig Matilda for eating up my wife's flower garden."

"He thinks one party will smooth over five years' worth of heartache he caused this town?" A stocky, elderly woman in Wranglers and pigtails asked.

"I don't trust that rascal any farther than I can throw him," a younger man in a motorized wheelchair exclaimed.

Then the entire café started talking at once, telling him about the underhanded stunts Peter had pulled, and all the problems he'd caused Kringle and its citizens.

He just listened.

Evan had no justification for what Peter had done the last time he was here. Although from a purely business standpoint, convincing the candy company to move to a bigger town had probably made sense. The Madisons probably had made a nice profit, and Evan knew that Peter had made a bundle off the deal.

But even one day in this small Texas town had shown Evan that the bottom line wasn't all that mattered. Moving that company had caused a lot of hardship. When they got back to Dallas, Evan planned to look into the specifics of the deal and make his own decision about what had happened.

At the moment, though, he wasn't sure he'd ever get out of the diner. Everyone had a story to tell.

Evan shot Chloe a look. Had she invited him here on purpose? Did she want him to hear these unsavory stories about his boss? She'd vetoed his suggestion to drive to Fort Worth to a nicer restaurant than what was available in the small town. Had that been intentional? Or was he attributing devious motives she didn't possess?

When the conversations dwindled and people finally wandered off, Evan looked at Chloe and raised one eyebrow. "That was, um...interesting."

She looked sheepish. "Sorry for being a bit underhanded, but I wanted you to understand exactly how your boss disrupted this entire town simply out of greed."

"You know I came on this trip with Peter to help him," he noted. "I don't control his actions."

"I respect your loyalty, but I hope you would stop him if he tried to do something terrible again."

As far as he knew, Peter was here to do exactly what he claimed—ask forgiveness and strive to have a perfect Christmas. "I'll try if that comes up."

But the apologies Peter owed the townsfolk didn't seem to be so quick and easy as his boss made them out to be.

"So tell me about this town," Evan said. "I'm Dallas born and bred. Teach me about how things work here. How did Kringle come into being?"

"They founded Kringle on the railroad like a lot of Texas small towns back in the late 1880s," Chloe explained. "The story goes that the people who settled here were Norwegian, and their leader's last name was Kringle. Then when Fort Worth grew, it syphoned off population from Kringle as people moved where the jobs were. During World War Two, to keep the town financially viable, the citizens capitalized on the name and went all in on Christmas tourism."

"Smart." Evan nodded.

"Each year at Christmas, it just kept getting bigger and bigger. Tourist visits from Thanksgiving through the New Year support our economy for the entire year, and Kringle Kandy was a big part of that success. Not only was the candy factory the town's biggest year-round employer, the Madisons also funded many of the holiday events. We've really had to scramble to make up for the loss."

"In what ways?" he asked, truly interested. The town fascinated him.

"On the outskirts of town, we have the Kringle Kampground and the Kringle Village, which at

Christmas features holiday-themed amusement rides, an indoor ice skating rink, and visits with Santa."

"Kringle Village? They couldn't think of a word that started with a K?" He chuckled.

Chloe shook her head and grinned. "Nope. We love our kitsch in Kringle."

Evan couldn't help returning her grin. This town was something else.

"This place *is* different," he admitted. "And I've only been here one full day."

"But different in a nice way." Chloe bit into her HoHoHo burger and wriggled with delight.

Evan turned his attention to his food. Truthfully, he wasn't sure about life in Kringle, at least not for someone like him. Having this many people know your every move was disconcerting. But it seemed to work for Chloe. She'd greeted everyone in the café when they'd entered, and she knew everyone, and they knew her.

In Dallas, he didn't even know the names of the people who lived on either side of his condo.

After they finished eating—the veggie burger was pretty darn good and the fries that accompanied it were out of this world—he paid the bill, and they headed for the door. Getting to that door, though, took time because Chloe stopped to say goodbye to everyone. In two cases, that caused the person to regale him once more about the negative impact Peter Thomas had had on their lives.

Overwhelmed, Evan felt exhausted by the time they finally reached the sidewalk outside the café.

"Sorry about that," Chloe murmured.

"Not your fault. Meeting the townsfolk was educational. I really had no idea Peter had caused so much harm. He didn't share any of this with me, Chloe, but you have to realize he's my boss, and I don't control his actions."

"But you can control who you work for."

"I don't see him in the same light you do."

Chloe sighed and couldn't meet his gaze. "I know. It was unfair of me to dump all this on you, but you seem like someone who would care."

Evan would like to think he was that sort of person. He tried to handle his life and work with integrity and ethics. Still, he couldn't guarantee that any business decision he'd made hadn't affected other people. Business was business.

"Would you like to take a stroll around the town square?" she invited. "Then you can walk me to my mom's house, then walk back for your car. We're only two blocks from home."

The night was warm for December, comfortable in the upper fifties. Why not?

"I haven't had my daily exercise," he said. "Let's do it."

They walked side by side, stopping to peek into

store windows. They decorated every business on the square to the hilt with over-the-top Christmas themes. Twinkle lights winked from every building. Christmas music played from speakers inset into the old limestone courthouse in the middle of the square, and in the air he could smell the scent of cinnamon, yeast bread, and wood smoke.

"You work out every day?"

"I have to," he said, patting his flat belly. "I have a mostly sedentary job. I'd turn to jelly if I didn't hit the gym every morning at five a.m. for ninety minutes of a high-intensity workout."

"Sounds brutal."

"Actually, I miss it when I don't."

"You like routine."

"I wouldn't say 'like' it as much as it's just part of my lifestyle."

"That's what I love about my job." Her eyes sparkled. "Every day is different. At the vet clinic, you never know what interesting thing will walk through those doors. And I get a workout lifting animals all day."

He stopped at a snowman family displayed in the window of an old-fashioned hardware store. He thought Amazon and big box warehouse stores had put places like this out of business. Grinning, he said, "This town is something special."

"This is nothing. Stick around for the full court Kringle press. We'll have a parade down Main Street and around Santa Boulevard on Saturday morning, along with the Christmas craft fair at city hall. The craft fair alone brings in people from all over the state. We even got a write up about it in Texas Monthly."

"Christmas sounds like an excellent business plan," he noted. "A great way to maximize earning potential."

She laughed softly, and he had to admit, it was appealing. He could definitely get used to her laughter. "I knew you'd like the way we turned Christmas into our main economy."

"Tell me more about Chloe," he said. "What do you do for fun?"

"I like reading," she said. "To me, there's nothing more relaxing than curling up with a good book. It's hard to find a nice chunk of time without distractions, especially this time of year. I take long bubble baths just so I can have twenty minutes of uninterrupted reading."

"Who interrupts you?"

Chloe waved a hand. "There is always some kind of pet emergency. Plus, I have friends galore who hate to see me sitting home in the evenings. They don't get that I cherish my alone time with my books."

"I'm a big reader too," he admitted.

"Really?" Her eyes brightened. "What are you into?"

"I like history and biographies, mostly. You?"

"I'm a fiction buff." Her cheeks pinked. "Romantic stories are my favorite, but mysteries are a close second."

He slanted her a sideways glance. "So you're a romantic at heart?"

"Hey." She met his grin with one of her own. "Have to be romantic to live in this town and survive."

"Well, from where I stand, you've done a fine job of not only surviving but thriving."

"That's kind of you to say." She dropped her gaze, then glanced over her shoulder at her mother's house behind them. "I had an enjoyable time tonight, Evan."

Evan was reluctant to see the evening end, but he had no reason to keep her. "Me too."

"Be sure and check on Vixen when you get back to the house." Chloe opened the front door. "Call me if there's any problem."

He agreed, and then they stepped over the threshold. Both Ruby and Peter turned to look at them and said simultaneously, "Hey, you're under the mistletoe."

Evan glanced up. Mistletoe hung in the middle of the doorway, and he was certain it hadn't been there when they'd left for dinner two hours ago.

"You have to kiss," Ruby said.

"Dirty pool, Mom. You put that up after we left."

Her mother widened her eyes, trying to look innocent, but then she burst out laughing.

Still, they were standing under mistletoe, regardless of why it was there. Evan turned to look at Chloe, who simply shrugged.

He leaned down.

Visibly, she quivered, and he could read the question in her eyes. Was he really going to kiss her?

Yes, ma'am, I am.

Evan's mouth hovered above hers. He could smell her sweet scent—yeast bread and Christmas and happiness all rolled into one.

His heart galloped, and she moistened her lips. He ignored the voice in the back of his brain that yelled, *don't do it*.

Gently, his lips brushed hers.

A brushfire flamed through him, bathing him from head to toe in pulsating heat, and he never wanted it to end. Without thinking, he pulled her closer, and she wrapped her arms around his neck. He could have gone on kissing her until the end of time if her mother and Peter weren't watching them.

Reluctantly, Evan let her go and straightened.

Chloe's eyes grew wide, and she reached up to finger her lips, looking as stunned as he felt from the impact of their kiss.

Oh, no. Oh wow. This was bad. A big mistake.

He was way too attracted to her. She was someone who had deep roots in this town, and he was just here for a couple of weeks. Getting involved with her would be bad for both of them. Long-distance relationships never worked. Worse, why was he even thinking about a relationship?

"G-good night," he stammered, then turned and ran out the door before he did something really foolish, like kiss her all over again.

CHAPTER 4

HOLY COW.

That kiss sure had been something. Mind-blowing was an understatement. She reeled, confused and hoping...

For what?

Chloe shook her head. She had no idea what she'd been hoping for. Evan had run out of her mother's house as if his hair was on fire, and Peter followed soon after. Leaving her with her mother.

Mom's eyebrows arched to her forehead, and a knowing smile lit her lips. Chloe kissed her mother's cheek and got out of there before she started asking her questions that Chloe didn't want to answer.

Once she got home, she took off her coat and sank against the door, realizing one scary thing. She liked Evan Conner. She liked him *a lot*. Probably too much. Kissing him had only confirmed her attraction to him.

But chemistry didn't mean a thing.

Sure, Evan *seemed* like a nice guy, and he definitely got her pulse racing, but that wasn't enough to build a relationship on. Or even a romantic fantasy.

"Cool your jets, Anderson," she muttered under her breath. "So what if he's hot as a firecracker and can kiss like the dickens? Big deal."

She had a life in Kringle, and he was just passing through. He'd told her enough about himself over dinner for her to realize his career meant everything to him. It seemed every member of his family was educated and successful. His brother had an MBA and worked for a large computer firm, while his sister was the CFO of a major cosmetics company.

Face it. He was out of her league.

Although her vet clinic kept her busy and made more than enough for her to live in Kringle, she knew it was small potatoes compared to what Evan and his siblings earned. If she considered the student loans that she was still paying—and would pay for many years—her income wasn't all that much.

But it was plenty for her. Kringle made her happy. If two years at the corporate clinic in Tyler had taught her nothing else, it was that happiness was more important than money. She'd been paid well there, but there were so many clients, she couldn't learn the names of all the patients or their pet parents. It had required her to keep each visit as short as possible and to sell additional treatments, whether pets really needed them. Many days, she'd felt like she was examining animals on a conveyor belt, and she hated it.

All that changed when her father passed away. Suddenly, appreciating each day and finding happiness had become the most important thing to her. Then, when her mother moved to Kringle a year after her father's death, Chloe moved with her. They both adored their adoptive town as passionately as any native.

Happy to be home, she plunked down on her favorite comfy chair and picked up Snowball, her rescue dog. Snowball was part Bichon Frise, and part who-knew-what. Chloe's best guess was a dash of Pomeranian, and a dab of Maltese as well, but whatever her heritage, Snowball was the perfect name for her.

Chloe discovered her on a cold and snowy morning, huddled in the clinic's doorway and tied to the doorknob. Someone had left her there. It had taken a moment for Chloe to realize that the pile of white fluff in the corner was a dog and not a clump of snow, hence the name Snowball.

Snowball had been skinny, sickly, and frightened. Chloe had taken her inside and nursed her back to health. Instantly, Snowball bonded to her. She was a wonderful, loving dog who brought joy to Chloe's life every single day. Even though she'd been living with Chloe for two years, she still was slow to warm up to strangers though, especially men. But once she decided you were okay, then your lap was hers from then on out.

Stroking the dog, Chloe told her about the date with Evan and the kiss. "What do you think? Should I just stay away from him? Or could I enjoy this feeling while it lasts, putting no expectations on an outcome?"

Snowball thumped her tail against Chloe's thigh.

"I see. So you approve of him, do you? But what if I can't keep things casual? What if I spend time with him, and I get my heart broken when he leaves town? What then, Snowball?"

As usual, the dog had no sage advice. She was a superb listener, but not much on offering concrete solutions.

"I know you know the right answer," Chloe teased, patting the dog. "You just want to me to figure it out on my own."

Because avoiding Evan completely wasn't an option. She'd already promised to stop by the Madison house every day to check on Vixen. And she always kept her promises. But next time, she was going to look up before she went through a doorway. No more getting ambushed by mistletoe!

* * *

"What do you think?" Peter asked, his tone, as usual, a little demanding. This morning, Peter had come down to breakfast, laptop in hand, ready to decide about the party.

Evan scrolled through Kringle Kakes website filled with specialty cakes and realized he didn't care. A cake was a cake. Although maybe kakes were different?

"Any cake is fine," he said, returning the laptop to Peter. "You could even consider cupcakes and get a bunch of different flavors."

"Cupcakes aren't impressive enough." His boss shook his head. "It has to be special."

As had become their habit, every decision about the party turned into a debate. Peter wanted a lavish party. Trying to impress the people of Kringle with his wealth, which Evan thought was tacky. Peter had come here to make amends for taking away the livelihood of many of the residents. It seemed to Evan that the worst thing he could do now was flaunt his wealth in their faces.

Sadly, Peter didn't see it that way. "That cake has got to make a statement. I want something that will knock everyone's socks off." Peter scrolled through the pictures a few more times, then landed on a picture near the end. "This one. I'll see if they can make it look like a Christmas cake and also add a few extra layers."

Evan didn't have to be psychic to know which cake Peter had chosen. It would be the super gigantic wedding cake, the one that cost the most. The thing was already massive. Adding a few more layers was going to make it gargantuan. The only positive about this was that Peter's order would bring in a nice profit for Kringle Kakes bakery.

"Okay. We'll go there and order it in person," Evan said. "I don't think it's possible to explain what you want through the website."

Peter seemed happy with the plan.

"We'll go over there after you do your walk on the treadmill for an hour." Part of Evan's job was riding herd on Peter to make sure he did his cardiac exercise regimen.

For once, Peter didn't argue. He simply shrugged and headed off to the exercise room.

While Peter worked out, Evan went to check on Vixen and found her cuddled in the corner, nursing her babies.

Vixen looked up at him with big brown moony eyes as if she was madly in love with him and thumped her tail enthusiastically.

Evan's heart skipped a beat, and his chest got hot, and a melting sensation slid through his veins. He couldn't deny that the dog and her pups were growing on him.

Crouching, he reached over to scratch Vixen behind the ears.

Her tail thumped all the harder.

The puppies were so young their eyes weren't open yet. One of the tiny babies had squirmed himself away from his mother. He raised his head and whimpered softly, his little nose twitching as he sought to find her with his sense of smell.

Evan was learning a lot about newborn puppies. They didn't look a thing like an older puppy. They were so small and helpless. He'd avoided touching them and letting Vixen care for them.

He moved from a crouch to a seated position, landing on his bottom beside the dog bed. He watched them for a moment, studying how Vixen gently licked her babies and herded them to her side with a paw.

The doorbell rang, snapping him out of his reverie.

That had to be Chloe. She'd been stopping by every morning on her way to work and then again on her way home. He'd started looking forward to this twice daily ritual. Three days had passed since their date—and that mind-blowing kiss—but they'd both pretended it hadn't happened.

They were forming a friendship, but that's all it was.

"It's enough," he mumbled under his breath, trying to convince himself. "It's enough."

He hopped up and rushed to the front door, unable to contain the big smile pushing up the sides of his mouth. He flung open the door to find Chloe standing there with a big grin of her own.

Like most days, she dressed for work in a nice blouse and slacks, covered with her lab coat. He enjoyed seeing her dressed as a vet, but a part of him missed that elf outfit. She'd looked extra cute as an elf.

Whoa, had he just thought that? Was he getting bitten by the Kringle Christmas fever?

"Hi!" She greeted him breathlessly, her cheeks pinked from the blustery weather, her soft brown hair windblown and sexily disheveled.

"Hey." His eyes caught her gaze and held it.

"How are you this morning?"

That was something else he liked about Chloe. She didn't just ask about Vixen and the puppies. She asked about him as well, and she seemed genuinely interested in the answer.

"I'm doing well. You?"

Her grin widened. "It would be *impossible* for me to be any better."

Oh wow, he loved her wildly contagious optimism. Wished he could bottle it and take it back home with him to Dallas.

"This way," he said, leading her down the hall to check on Vixen.

"How is the party planning going?" she asked.

Evan shook his head and rolled his eyes. "Over-the-top. You should see the cake he's picked out. It should be impressive. But I might not stand next to it because even though I'm six feet tall, I'm pretty sure it will tower over me."

Chloe laughed. "The last thing any of us needs is for an imposing cake to make us feel shorter."

"True." He chuckled, his heart feeling fizzy.

In the den, Chloe sank down on her knees beside the dog bed to examine Vixen and her puppies. "They look great. You're doing a fabulous job. I think I'll just come by once a day now. You've got this."

His fizzy heart went flat. "You have way too much confidence in my pet care abilities."

"And you don't have nearly enough confidence in it." Chloe shook her head, dusted her palms together, and got to her feet. "You're a natural at this."

"I feel like a fraud."

"Then you're doing an excellent job of faking it until you make it. Keep up the outstanding work." She chucked him lightly on his upper arm.

It was no big deal. Barely a touch, but his nerve endings came alive, tingly and thrilling, and Evan forgot to breathe.

"Our big Christmas parade is tomorrow. Do you plan to go?"

Was she asking him out? The tingling spread over this entire body, along with a carpet of goosebumps.

"Um."

"You haven't lived until you've seen the Kringle Christmas parade. If Peter really wants to have a perfect Christmas, he needs to be there."

Evan had heard something about the parade, but he hadn't made plans to go. Not even with Peter. Parades really weren't his thing. Even as a child, he hadn't found them interesting. This weekend, he'd hoped to get some work done. But if Chloe was asking him out, did he really want to miss out on a chance to spend more time with her?

"I've got work to catch up on."

"All weekend? You can't take off for two hours to watch most of Kringle act silly?" she wheedled. "We all have a lot of fun."

He was pretty sure she was asking him out. "Are you going?"

"I'm in the parade," she said. "My clinic sponsors a float along with the Kringle Kritters Rescue Society."

He couldn't resist asking, "Will you dress as an elf?"

She laughed and nodded. "Yep. Santa and Mrs. Claus will be there as well. Plus, you can meet my staff and my friends and a few of our best behaved Kringle Kritters."

The elf costume convinced Evan to attend. He wouldn't miss that for the world.

"I'll talk to Peter and see if he wants to go," he said.

"Maybe I'll see you there."

Their eyes met again, and she gave him a coy smile. "I should go."

"Will you be back tonight?"

She shook her head. "Vixen and the puppies are doing so well. I'll drop by tomorrow morning instead."

"I see."

"Of course," Chloe said, eyeing him speculatively. "I don't know what will happen to her once the pups wean and you and Peter have left town. Vixen and the puppies need forever homes."

Evan hadn't thought that far ahead. "Won't she go back to her owner?"

Chloe shook her head. "Her previous owner passed away, remember? Vixen and her puppies will go to the local rescue organization, Kringle Kritters, and hopefully…" She crossed her fingers. "Someone will adopt them. They need someone kind who loves dogs and will give them a great forever home."

Evan hadn't been first in his class at law school for nothing. He knew when he was being played. "I can't adopt Vixen, Chloe, for lots of reasons. I live in a condo in Dallas. I'm always at work. I simply don't have time for a pet."

She didn't even try to pretend that she hadn't been trying to talk him into adopting Vixen or one of her puppies. "Are you sure? You're so good with them."

He liked Vixen. A lot. And these past few days with her puppies had convinced him that he really was a dog lover, but he wasn't kidding about his lifestyle being wrong for a pet. His work was everything to him.

"I work constantly," he went on, realizing he was trying to convince himself as much as her. "And travel frequently. Days off are nonexistent. My job truly is twenty-four seven."

"You never have a day off?" She blinked, looking astounded.

"Ever. I work holidays and weekends, and until this trip with Peter, I hadn't taken a vacation in five years. Even now, I'm only here because Peter's health is iffy, and he needed someone to look out for him."

"So, you're his personal nursemaid too?"

"Looking after Peter is part of my job description. Plus, as I've said, I'm rarely home, which means I'd have to put Vixen in daycare all day, every day. She deserves a better life than that."

Chloe's unwavering gaze was a punch to the stomach. "Seems to me that you deserve a better life than that as well. Everyone needs time off to recharge their batteries."

Her comment caught him off guard. He guessed on the surface, his life might seem less than perfect, but he was used to working long days with not much rest. Until this trip with Peter, he couldn't remember the last time he'd had a day off.

"Financial success takes a lot of commitment and sacrifices," he mumbled. Was he looking for excuses?

"I don't believe that having financial success means trading in your free time for money. There's more to life than work, work, work. What about family and friends and hobbies?"

Evan knew that a small-town vet probably couldn't understand how he felt. He'd dedicated his entire life to achieving a certain level of financial freedom. His parents had pushed him throughout his life. Rewarding him when he succeeded and withholding their approval when he did not. He was proud of what he'd accomplished, even if it meant he'd given up most of his personal life.

He wasn't quite sure how to explain it, but he tried. "Chloe, being focused on a career isn't a bad thing."

"It isn't," she said, sadness lacing her voice. "What's a bad thing is when work takes over your life. Are you happy, Evan?"

He'd never really thought about it before, but now that she asked, the answer that immediately popped into his mind was not what he said. "Yes, sure, of course."

"Do you ever think about what would make you happy?"

"I'm happy." He said it too forcefully. Too intensely.

She arched her eyebrows. "In what ways?"

"Huh?"

"In what ways are you happy?"

He didn't know how to answer her. On paper, he should be happy. He'd accomplished everything he'd set out to do. He had a successful career. He had a lot of money. He had a nice condo. He'd achieved most of the awards given out in his field. They had featured him on the cover of D magazine.

"I can buy anything I want whenever I want it."

"And that makes you happy?"

"It gives me freedom."

Her smile was wistful. "Freedom to work twenty-four seven? That sounds like a prison to me."

"I love my work."

"Even the part that includes babysitting Peter Thomas?"

"Well..." He chuckled. "No job is perfect."

"Where do you see yourself long term?" Chloe prodded. "All alone in a mansion sitting on an enormous pile of money like Scrooge?"

"That's not fair."

"Isn't it?" She canted her head. "You told me you

live to work and make money. If that's the path you're on, it's likely that's where you'll end up."

He still didn't see what was wrong about amassing wealth. *It's not the wealth that's the problem,* whispered a voice at the back of his head. *It's the forsaking of everything else to achieve it.*

"You should think about your future in terms of more than just money." She jammed her hands into the pocket of her lab coat. "Who will be in your life ten years from now? Twenty? Will you be like Peter? All alone?"

"No!" he said it so forcefully that Chloe took a step back. Lowering his voice, he said, "I didn't mean for that to come out sounding so harsh."

He knew she was right. For years he'd focused on his career to the exclusion of everything else, but now that he'd spent some time in Kringle, and with Chloe, he realized he was missing out on a lot of important things.

He'd only been here a few days, but he'd already enjoyed things he'd never even considered before. He enjoyed going for walks through Kringle and meeting the residents. He'd also come to enjoy exploring the eclectic assortment of shops on what passed for downtown Kringle.

"I think attending the parade sounds great," he said, deciding that work could wait. Not much happened around the holidays anyway, and he wanted to see Chloe in that elf costume again. "I'll convince Peter to go. But isn't it over pretty quickly?"

Chloe laughed and patted him on the arm. "You're in for a big surprise. This parade pulls in visitors from all over Texas. Tiny Kringle will not be tiny tomorrow. It will overflow with people. In fact, you and Peter should head downtown early tomorrow with some lawn chairs and snag yourself a good viewing spot before they're all gone. Crowds start grabbing the prime spots at sunrise."

"You're kidding? For a small-town parade?"

"You have no idea." She grinned. "People love this parade. It's filled with goofy floats and silly characters, and it's all so much fun."

Evan figured he'd try it. "Sure. We'll come. I must go buy some chairs today. I don't think this house has any lawn chairs."

"Don't worry. You and Peter can go with my mom," Chloe offered. "She has plenty of chairs. She also can narrate the parade so that you know who everyone is."

Her offer was very nice, and Evan hoped her mother didn't mind. It would be fun to have someone give them the inside scoop.

"You sure she won't mind?"

"She'll love it." She cast a glance at him. "If you're not too busy, maybe you can come by the clinic and help us out with our float this evening."

"I don't mind helping, but I'm not really handy

with tools," he admitted. "I'm not sure how much help I'll be."

"You can glue paper on the float. It doesn't take any skills and bring Peter. He can use that time to show the people of Kringle how he's changed. He really hasn't talked to many of them yet. Most of the people I've spoken to at the clinic haven't seen him since he returned."

"I know." Evan realized Peter wasn't doing his part.

His boss had supposedly come to Kringle to apologize and have what he'd called the perfect Kringle Christmas, but he'd spent the last few days holed up in his room, working on the computer.

"I'll talk to Peter tonight. I'm sure we can stop by and help."

Chloe rewarded him with a bright smile. He loved the way she smiled. It was sincere and appealing and always made him smile back.

"That's great." She gave him the address to her clinic, and her cell phone number and then headed for the front door.

"Don't blame me, though, if I make a mess. I have warned you about my lack of mechanical skills."

"I'm willing to take the risk," she assured him.

When they reached the foyer, she opened the front door, glanced up, and with a short wave, scurried out. Evan knew what she was doing. Since the kiss, they both avoided getting stuck together in a doorway, mistletoe or not.

He might be smart enough to tell when she was trying to convince him to adopt Vixen, but he wasn't smart enough to resist falling for Chloe.

He would have to keep their relationship on a friendship-only level. When he returned to Dallas with Peter, he didn't want to owe anyone in Kringle an apology, especially Chloe.

CHAPTER 5

"YOU NEED to make the spots bigger, and we should scatter them around."

Evan glanced at the young girl who was standing by his right arm in front of the float that he was decorating in the rear parking lot of Chloe's vet clinic.

The girl looked to be around ten, with sandy hair and bright-blue eyes. She had her hands on her hips and a *you're-a-dufus* expression on her face.

"What?" he asked.

"You put the spots in a straight line." She shook her head. "You're doing it *all* wrong."

"I am?" Evan glanced at his work.

So far, he'd only stuck four large black round spots onto the float, and now that he looked at them, they were in a line.

Someone had assigned him the job of cutting out and gluing black construction paper spots to the white butcher paper wrapped around a pickup truck. The front part of the truck was being decorated by Chloe and a woman who worked for her named Suzannah. The kid belonged to Suzannah.

Chloe and Suzannah were decorating the front of the pickup as the head and ears of a dalmatian, and he was working on the dog's sides and back. It promised to look really cute, if he stopped pasting the spots in a row.

The girl watched as Evan glued it to a fifth spot. She sighed and shook her head as if he were a hopeless case.

He stopped and looked at her.

"I gather this isn't right either," he said, struggling to resist the urge to laugh.

The girl was so serious. "You're terrible at this," she said. "Dalmatians don't have spots that go in lines. They are everywhere. Like when you have a rash."

Evan couldn't stop himself. He laughed and conceded the point. "You're right. I am bad at this." He tipped his head and studied his work. "Any ideas how we can fix it?"

The girl bobbed his head. "Sure. I can help you. I'm really good at this. I'll go get more black paper. We can put lots of little spots around the big spots you glued so they look okay. Be right back."

After the child ran off, Suzannah, the girl's mother, walked over from where she was working on the front of the truck and smiled sheepishly at Evan.

"I'm sorry about Abby's brutal honesty," she said. "I've been trying to teach her how to be politely truthful, but it doesn't seem to work. She's nailed the being truthful part. Not so the polite."

"She's right, though. I'm bad at this." Evan chuckled. "I've never decorated a float before."

Suzannah looked at him as if he's grown three heads. "Not even when you were a kid?"

He shook his head. "My family stressed academics over recreational pursuits."

She clicked her tongue at that but didn't comment on it. "Let's see if we can move a few of those spots."

Thankfully, since the glue was still damp, they could shift two of the spots, so they were no longer in a row.

Peter had gone off with Ruby to begin his apology mission to the citizens of the town, leaving Evan to decorate the float with Chloe and her friends.

Speaking of Chloe, where had she gotten off to?

Evan glanced across the parking lot and saw Chloe and Abby headed toward him and Suzannah.

They carried additional black paper, which he assumed was for more spots on the float. The two of them were chattering and laughing, having a great time.

Seeing Chloe reminded him why, at least for him, coming to Kringle hadn't been a bad idea. He was glad he'd come and glad he'd met her. She was special, and he knew that long after he left this town, he'd remember her.

Thinking about leaving Kringle bothered him, and he must have been frowning when Chloe and Abby walked up because they both looked at each other and burst out laughing.

"What is it?" he asked.

"You look like Scrooge," Abby said.

"Bah humbug to you too." He glanced at Chloe. "Did Abby tell you that I'm doing a poor job?"

Chloe grinned big and, as usual, whenever he was around her, Evan smiled. Whenever he was around her, he felt lighter somehow. Happy.

"Abby reported your failings." Chloe shook her head and muted her grin. To Abby she said, "I know you warned me, but I had no idea that you were being so accurate. Thank goodness you were here to see what had happened and correct things."

Abby beamed at the praise. "Told you that you were goofing up."

Evan hung his head, pretending to look contrite.

"It's not your fault you're no good at this," Abby said, trying to make him feel better. "I've been helping Dr. Anderson since I was little. She says I'm the best worker she has. When I grow up, I'm going to be a vet just like her."

"Is that so?" Evan smiled at first Abby and then Chloe. "Good job. Keep helping. You can learn a lot from Dr. Anderson."

"That's all Abby's ever wanted to be," Suzannah said. "I better start saving for vet school pronto."

"Yes. You'll want to get a definite head start," he said, stopping himself at the last moment from offering her additional financial advice. Suzannah hadn't asked for his input.

Chloe hugged Abby. "You'll make a great vet, and you're one of the best workers I have each year, but remember, everyone is a good worker because they are donating their time to help. We appreciate everyone's help. Even people who might not be the best at knowing how to glue on spots on a dalmatian."

"How about you show me how?" Evan asked Abby. "We want this to be the best float in the parade. It represents Dr. Anderson and her clinic."

"You betcha!" Abby plunked onto the asphalt and started cutting out black dots of varying sizes from the construction paper.

Her mother returned to the front of the truck to finish working on her part of the project, so Evan joined Abby at the bed. But instead of rejoining Suzannah, Chloe came over to them. The scissors Chloe provided were new, so it was easy to cut through the construction paper quickly. The three of them worked together. Evan cutting out the spots and Chloe dabbing on the glue before handing them to Abby, who placed them on the float.

Evan couldn't remember the last time he'd done something simply for the fun of it. He spent his time on emails, phone calls, and contracts. Meetings, workshops, and travel dominated his life, and while he enjoyed the challenges of business, it had been a long time since he'd just relaxed and let himself play at something that didn't really matter.

The float was turning out to be very cute. It really looked like a dalmatian wearing a Santa hat.

"Who rides in the truck's bed?" Evan asked.

"Abby will ride in the back with me," Chloe said. "One of my vet techs, Stanley, will drive. This is his truck. His two dalmatians will ride in the front seat with him. They love people."

"Dr. Anderson and I will dress as elves," Abby said.

"Where will Santa and Mrs. Claus ride?" he asked.

"They'll be on a different float." Abby leaned forward and whispered to Evan, "My mom is Mrs. Claus this year, and her best friend, Zach Delaney, is playing Santa."

Evan didn't know who Zach Delaney was, but he glanced at Abby's mother, Savannah. She was young, slender, and pretty. She didn't look a thing like how he envisioned Mrs. Claus should look. But hey, what did he know? A lot of things in this town baffled him.

Maybe they planned to dress her up—or in this case, dress her down—so that she looked like an elderly woman.

They finished up the floats, and time flew by. Before Evan knew it, darkness had encroached on their party, and everyone was saying goodbye and drifting to their vehicles to head home.

Leaving just him and Chloe standing in the parking lot.

"Hey." He smiled at her. "Want to grab some dinner?"

She shook her head. "Sorry, I can't. I've already got a date."

"Oh." Evan felt as if she'd kicked him squarely in the gut. He shouldn't have been jealous, but dang if he wasn't. "I see. Well, have a delightful time."

"It's a date with my cousin and his family. They're in town for the parade."

Relief washed over him.

"You know, I could ask him if it's okay for you to join us." Her smiled warmed him up like hot chocolate on a cold winter morning.

"No, no." He waved away her invitation. "Go. Enjoy your family. I'll see you tomorrow."

Chloe's smiled softened, and she wriggled her fingers. "Good night and thanks so much for helping us out today."

"It was my pleasure," he said, and realized that he absolutely meant it.

"I had fun."

"Me too."

"Until tomorrow?"

"I'm looking forward to it," Evan said, and wondered what it would be like to wake up to her beatific smile every day for the rest of his natural life.

* * *

"This parade is even lamer than I remembered," Peter grumped as they watched the Kringle Hardware float go by. They rigged the trailer to look like a giant hammer with people dressed as nails riding on it. "These floats are terrible."

Evan had to use all his self-control to avoid saying something rude to his boss. Peter was in a real mood today, complaining about anything and everything. Since the parade had started, all he'd done was gripe.

Honestly? Evan loved the kitsch and whimsy of the local parade. From the Kringle Memorial Hospital float complete with employees in scrub suits and stethoscopes dancing clumsily but enthusiastically to "Bad Case of Loving You," to the Kringle Karate Akademy float with participants dressed in gis and performing slow motion tai chi, to the Kringle Koffee Klatch float featuring a giant platter of chocolate chips and an oversized coffee cup to match. Despite its amateurish simplicity, the parade—and the town—had such heart.

They'd met Ruby at seven, and people were

already lining the road. She'd snagged them a great viewing location smack in the middle of Kringle Avenue, the major thoroughfare leading to the town square. She'd set up lawn chairs in front of the Kringle Library so that they all had a comfy place to sit.

"Hot chocolate?" Ruby asked, holding the thermos and paper cups she'd brought with her.

"Not unless it's got whiskey in it," Peter said.

"You can't have alcohol," Evan said automatically. "Doctor's orders."

Peter glowered at him.

"Hot chocolate?" Ruby repeated. "I have peppermint sticks to stir it with."

"I'll take some," Evan said. Not because he really wanted any hot chocolate, but more because Peter was acting like such a stick-in-the-mud when Ruby was bending over backward to be nice.

Evan still found her attitude toward her ex-fiancé surprising. She didn't seem to have any bitterness about what Peter had done to her or the town. She also seemed fairly immune to Peter's snipes and complaints about the parade. She also seemed to be immune to the stream of flattery he directed her way. Maybe now that she knew what he was capable of, she took nothing he said seriously.

"We should attend the amusement park tomorrow and do some sledding," she suggested.

Evan glanced around. It was cooler today than it

had been the last few days, but there wasn't a speck of snow in sight. What was she talking about, sledding? "How?"

"The sledding is indoors." She smiled knowingly. "Kringle Village makes artificial snow."

"Sounds ingenious. And like a lot of fun." He turned to Peter. "What do you think? Maybe you can run into more of the citizens at Kringle Village. Some people you might have missed last night."

Peter shrugged. "I guess, but I'm more focused on the party these days. I think I've talked with enough folks that they realize that me advising the Madisons to move their candy shop to Dallas was just business. Now that it's been a few weeks since my heart attack, I realize I may have overreacted. I did what any good businessman would do—I saw an opportunity, and I took it. Nothing wrong with that."

Evan felt as if Peter had thrown a bucket of cold ice water on his face. "What are you talking about?"

"I need not apologize for doing what made good business sense," Peter waved a dismissive hand. "I don't know why I thought I did."

"You had a massive heart attack that caused you to reevaluate the way you were living your life," Evan reminded him. "You realized how much you'd stepped on the backs of the people in this town to make more money."

"I didn't step on anyone's back," Peter denied.

Gobsmacked, Evan stared at his boss open-mouthed. Since when had his attitude changed? They still had another week in Kringle, and this entire trip had been his idea. Making amends was his entire reason for being here.

Or so it had been.

So much for changing. Since he'd started feeling better, Peter was turning back into his old self.

Although Evan was glad his boss' health improved, he was sorry to see him revert to his old, selfish ways. Peter had sounded so sincere when he had talked about apologizing to the people of Kringle and making it up to the people he'd hurt, that Evan couldn't help feeling disappointed.

His boss wasn't the man Evan had thought he was trying to become.

He glanced at Ruby, who was sitting between him and Peter. If Peter disappointed her, she didn't show it. She made no comment about it and instead told them about each float as it passed by as if Peter had said nothing.

They represented quite a few local companies, including the local bakery, Kringle Kakes. Peter launched into an overview of the small, family-owned bakery and its potential for growth as the float slowly rolled by.

"You seem to know a lot about Kringle Kakes," Evan pointed out, curious why his boss was so well-informed.

Peter didn't answer, and Evan wasn't sure

whether it was because he didn't want to or because the parade had gotten loud again.

Chloe's pet float was passing by, and Evan stood to get a better look. Next to him, Ruby was cheering on the small truck, waving her hands and calling out, "Go Chloe!" Inside the truck, next to the driver, sat two dalmatians. They had their heads partway out of the passenger window, barking gleefully.

In the back of the truck, Chloe and Abby sat on chairs and tossed candy to the children. A Christmas carol featuring dogs barking played loudly from the truck's stereo, causing laughter from the audience.

Abby and Chloe dressed as elves, and as Evan had noticed the last time that he'd seen her dressed this way, Chloe made a very cute elf.

She waved at him and her mother as the truck passed by. It was funny how proud Evan felt about the float. Objectively, there was nothing special about it. It was just a regular pickup truck dressed up to look like a dog. But he'd had fun decorating it, and in his opinion, it was the best float in the parade.

Once the float passed by them, Ruby sat back down, and Evan followed suit. He hadn't noticed before, but Peter had remained sitting the entire time.

"Are you feeling okay?" Evan asked.

"Fine." Peter pursed his lips.

"Why didn't you stand for Chloe's float?"

"I just don't see a lot to cheer about," Peter muttered. "It's just a truck with a few decorations."

Even though Evan had thought the same thing just a few moments ago, when Peter said it, the sentiment felt empty. Evan had to admit that Peter wasn't doing a lot to ensure that this trip turned out to be a perfect Christmas. He'd turned down several invitations to parties and get-togethers with people from the community, and now he was making it clear he could hardly wait to leave the parade.

Although they hadn't been friends back in Dallas, Evan had thought prior to this trip that he had a pretty good handle on what type of guy Peter was. But this experience showed him otherwise.

Right after the heart attack, Peter had seemed very sincere. Evan truly believed that he wanted to make amends.

But now, as each day rolled into the next, Evan wasn't so sure of Peter's sincerity anymore. His boss seemed focused only on the party, which wasn't a problem. What was bothersome was the *why*? Peter seemed to want to use the party to impress the residents of Kringle. He wanted to show off how much money he had, which wasn't at all why he said he'd come here.

Evan glanced at his boss, who was sitting in the lawn chair on the other side of Ruby. He wasn't even watching the parade. At the moment, a group of schoolchildren dressed as candy canes sang Christmas carols as they strolled by.

Peter never even looked up. He focused on his cell phone.

"Something I can help with?" Evan offered, looking directly at Peter. "You're supposed to be taking it easy and enjoying the trip. If it's work, I'll take care of it."

Peter shut off his phone and put it in his pocket. "It's nothing," he said with a shake of his head. "It's not work."

Evan had been an attorney for five years, and during that time, he'd developed a keen sense of people. He'd become pretty good at telling when someone was lying to him. In fact, his instincts were so good that he was rarely wrong.

Which is how he knew, with complete certainty, that Peter was lying.

CHAPTER 6

"PETER WANTS to go look at Christmas trees," Ruby said in the kitchen the next morning.

"What?" Was her mother getting involved with Peter Thomas again? An uneasy feeling rippled over her.

Ruby continued reading the news on her tablet computer and never looked up at her daughter. "I said yes. You're expected to come as well."

"Expected?" Chloe sank her hands on her hips.

"Peter would appreciate it if you'd join us," her mother amended. "And so would I."

"Okay." Chloe went to the breadbox, took out two slices of whole wheat bread, and dropped them into the toaster. Truthfully, she'd like to have a nice quiet day without Peter Thomas in it. The man annoyed her. He didn't seem a bit interested in the people of Kringle, no matter what he claimed.

Well, most of them anyway.

He definitely was interested in Ruby; that much was clear. Flirting with her mother was the only time Peter seemed to get off his phone.

Thankfully, though, Mom didn't seem to have the slightest interest in him. She was polite, but that was it. She didn't fawn or fuss over him like she'd once done, which Chloe felt was a splendid thing. He wasn't a nice man. She felt bad that he'd had a heart attack, but that didn't mean she was willing to overlook his glaring flaws.

Peter Thomas was an insincere phony. The only thing that perplexed her was what her mother had seen in him all those years ago, and why was she hanging out with him now.

Whatever qualities had attracted her mother to him back then were no longer visible. At least not to Chloe.

Her toast popped up, and Chloe topped it with smashed avocado. Then she joined her mother at the small bistro table near the window.

Growing up, breakfast had been a lively occasion. Her father loved breakfast, so he'd cook bacon, eggs, and hash browns most mornings. He wore a white, frayed apron that said, "Kiss the Cook," and made a big production about stealing a kiss from her mother.

Her dad passed away ten years ago, but Chloe

still missed him deeply. He'd been a kind-hearted man with a big laugh and unending love for his family. Exactly the sort of man she wanted to marry one day and raise a family with.

This time of the year, it was especially difficult. Her father, like her mother, had loved Christmas. He'd decorate the house from the top of the roof to the shrubs in the front yard and had their house glowing with lights and dancing Christmas figurines. Her mother teased that he was just a big kid at heart, but her father hadn't minded.

Instead, he'd grab her around the waist, dip her for a long kiss, and say, "Don't you forget it."

He'd been such a big softy too. He was the reason Chloe had become a vet. He'd brought home every stray that had ever crossed his path. He felt all creatures deserved a loving home, and his compassion didn't stop with animals. Every year, he bought the scrawniest Charlie Brown Christmas tree he could find just so it would have a home. He said he felt sorry for the tree and wanted it to be happy too.

Thinking about him now made her smile.

Slowly she chewed her toast, feeling nostalgia settle over her. She knew her mother missed her husband deeply. They'd been high school sweethearts who never spent a day apart until the day he died.

That kind of love was something Chloe was sure

Peter wouldn't understand. Having spent time with him, she was glad her mother hadn't married the man. Ruby deserved someone just as special as Chloe's father had been. Someone who truly adored her.

"You can go with Peter by yourself," Chloe said. "I need not tag along."

Ruby shook her head and looked directly at her daughter. "You're not getting out of this. You started all of this by stopping at the house to take care of Vixen, so you need to see it through. Besides, I know Evan is looking forward to seeing you."

Chloe figured now was a good time to talk things over with her mother. She didn't want her getting the wrong idea. "Don't try to matchmake."

"Was that what I was doing?" her mother asked, feigning innocence. She might have gotten away with it if her expression hadn't been so guilty.

Chloe sent her a chiding expression.

"I don't think I'm trying to matchmake. All I'm doing is pointing out that you were the one who agreed to make sure Peter had a perfect Kringle Christmas. You can't back out of that promise now. Ensure he has a great time."

"You can't hold me to that," she said. "I can't control other people's emotions."

"No, but you can set things up for the best probable outcome."

"We'll see," Chloe said, knowing she was being manipulated. "And for the record, you're the one who agreed, then you said *I* would help. That's what Evan calls being *volun-told*."

A suspicious smile appeared on Ruby's lips, and then humming a little, she went back to browsing her electronic device. Chloe decided not to argue. Her mother was a kind person who thought the best of everyone, and Chloe knew she wouldn't be able to convince her that they owed Peter nothing.

Path of least resistance, Chlo, she told herself. *Just get through this.*

Not that spending time with Evan was a hardship. Unlike Peter, who seemed focused only on himself, Evan was one of the nicest men Chloe had ever met, and he truly seemed to care about how his work affected people.

"I'll admit, Evan Conner is a very nice young man," Ruby said as if reading Chloe's mind.

"You are so obvious, Mom." Chloe laughed and shook her head. "I will not fall for Evan. Yes, he's a nice guy. And yes, I like spending time with him. But he lives and works in Dallas, and I have no intention of leaving Kringle. I have my business here, you're here, and my friends are here. This is home. I have no desire for an urban lifestyle."

"I guess time will tell." Ruby chuckled.

"No, it won't, Mom. Seriously, Evan and I are

just friends, and that's all we'll ever be. He has his own life. I have mine. We live a hundred miles apart. Our goals are different. Our values differ. Please don't make this out to be something it's not."

Ruby looked up from her tablet. She switched it off, then reached across the table and patted Chloe's hand. "Okay. I won't make it out to be something other than what it is."

With that, her mother left the room without promising not to meddle.

Her mother was clever. Very clever indeed.

* * *

"I want the biggest tree they have." Peter sauntered along the main aisle of the Christmas tree lot. "It has to be huge and perfect. No broken branches. No bare spots."

Evan sighed. Not again. This was their fourth tree lot in the past two hours. Each lot took them farther and farther from town, but no matter how many perfectly fine trees they saw, Peter wasn't happy.

He insisted on more, more, more. When was enough enough?

"If you get one that is too big, we won't be able to decorate it," Ruby pointed out. "Why not get one that is a reasonable height? That way, we can reach all of it, even the top."

The expression on Peter's face was priceless. He

scrunched up his face, widened his eyes, and bared his teeth like an upset dog. "I'll *hire* people to decorate the tree. I will not do it myself."

Evan and Chloe exchanged a look. Ruby seemed unruffled by Peter's impatience and huffy attitude.

In the cold air, Chloe's cheeks were adorably pink. She wore a white beret that matched her white down parka, and practical rubber boots perfect for the damp earth they were tramping around on. Evan wished he'd worn something wiser than his dress shoes, but the only other footwear he'd brought with him were his jogging sneakers.

Still grumbling, Peter moved down the row of trees, gesturing as he went. "In fact, all these tree lots should offer that service. You should be able to pay them to deliver, set up the tree, and then decorate it. They shouldn't expect their customers to do it. That sounds like a lot of work."

Evan barely resisted the impulse to groan. His boss really didn't get Christmas at all.

"Decorating it is the fun part," Chloe said. "And the merchants know that. Why would they want to take the joy away from their customers? Besides, how many people want someone else to decorate their tree?"

"Me," Peter said, as if the world revolved around his wants and needs. "They should have the service for people like me."

Evan had to bite his tongue to keep from telling his boss that he was acting like a jackass.

"Okay," Chloe conceded with a touch of acid in her voice. "Maybe a rich person from Dallas will pay someone to decorate his or her tree, but that's different. This is Kringle. We decorate our own trees here."

If Peter was listening to her, it didn't show. While Chloe had been talking, he walked ahead and kept looking at trees, muttering as he went. Nothing at this lot seemed to be what he wanted either.

"Well, we tried," Evan said to her. "I'm ready to wave the white flag and go buy an artificial tree."

Chloe slowly shook her head. "Why is he so difficult?" She looked at Peter for a moment and then turned her attention to Evan. "How do you stand working for him?"

He knew what she meant, but loyalty to his boss kept him from speaking his truth. He told her what he'd been trying to convince himself of for the last few months. "He's not a bad guy, Chloe."

"He's not a good guy either," she countered, then relented. "Okay, so maybe he's not *that* bad, but he is pretty self-absorbed. And he's dead wrong about Christmas trees and the people of Kringle."

"In what way?"

"No one expects a gigantic tree that's professionally decorated. They are coming to a house for a

Christmas party, not going to city hall in Dallas. He's looking at this party the wrong way. It's about bringing the community together. It's about fellowship, great food, friendly conversations, and enjoyable company."

Evan completely agreed. He nodded, but he knew Peter well enough to know that once he set his mind to something, very little dissuaded him.

"It's his money," Ruby said, walking up behind them. "If he wants to waste it on a professionally decorated tree, let him. He desires a tree like that will help him have the perfect Christmas."

After Ruby moved to catch up to Peter, Evan cast a sidelong glance at Chloe who had her hands tucked into her pockets. He admired the way her hair curled at her shoulders and how artfully she'd applied just the barest hint of makeup. "You know she's right."

"She usually is."

"If an immense tree is what Peter wants, then he should get one and pay people to decorate it for him," Evan said. "It sounds like this magnificent tree is part of the perfect Christmas he's created in his mind."

"But no such tree exists. I don't think any tree will ever be good enough for him."

"That's Peter's cross to bear. Not ours."

Beside him, Chloe sighed. "You're right, just like

Mom is. What *I* feel is perfect for Christmas doesn't matter. What's important is that Peter has the Christmas he wants. It may not be my type, but he wants what he wants. I have no place to judge what works for him."

Evan nodded in agreement. He didn't like the way Peter was preparing for the party. In his opinion, his boss was going about this the wrong way. But it wasn't up to him. He'd promised to help Peter when he'd come on this trip, and that's what he needed to do. He'd keep his opinions to himself.

"Since we've both had an epiphany, I guess we should help find this mythological tree so that we can head back to town before dark." Evan rubbed his palms together. "It's really starting to get cold."

"Agreed."

Evan guided Chloe toward another aisle from the one Peter and Ruby were in. Splitting up should speed things along. Hopefully.

He was walking so close to her that he could smell her delicious scent. A combo of cinnamon, vanilla, and sugar cookies. Her fragrance conjured imagines of hot chocolate sipped in front of a cozy fire. Which he'd never done before, but it sounded really nice right now.

"What kind of Christmas trees did you have growing up?" Chloe asked.

"We had an artificial one. The lights were already on it. You just stood it up and hung the ornaments," Evan said. "Pow! They did it in a flash. Mom said it was the only way to fly."

He expected her to disapprove, but she said, "That's handy."

Evan stopped walking and turned to look at her. "I'm surprised you feel that way. I thought you were a real tree kind of person."

Chloe shook her head. "No. I'm someone who believes people need to do what is right for them. Who am I to tell anyone how they should celebrate the holidays?"

He gave her a direct, unwavering look. "Um, weren't you the one telling Peter that the way he was approaching a tree was wrong?"

She waved her hands. "Yes. Yes. I know. I seem like a hypocrite. But Peter isn't buying a tree that brings him joy. He's buying a gigantic tree with the sole intent of impressing people. He's trying to make other people feel bad with his tree by showing them how rich he is. That's wrong."

Evan would like to defend his boss, but he couldn't. As far as he could tell, Chloe was right about Peter's motivation. He wasn't here to make amends as much as to show off.

This whole situation stunk. The people of Kringle deserved better. In the week Evan had been here, he'd found the citizens to be warm and helpful. They were even willing to understand why Peter did what he did with Kringle Kandy. What was the point of showing off his wealth?

Evan planned on talking to his boss when they got back to the house. He'd like to think that maybe Peter didn't realize how his behavior was coming across. He'd give him the benefit of the doubt and hope for the best.

At least for now.

Evan and Chloe wandered around the large Christmas tree lot for a few minutes. He wanted so badly to reach out and take her hand, but he didn't know if she'd like that or not, so he stuffed his hands in his pockets. Finally, a tree caught Evan's eye. It was a fir he could replant after the holidays.

Unfortunately, even though the concept was interesting, the poor pine tree had seen better days. It was truthfully sad-looking. Spindly and weak, the tree only stood two feet tall.

But he felt drawn to it.

He walked over and patted the tree, then he turned to Chloe. "If I buy this, can I plant it in your yard after the holidays?"

Chloe was standing still, staring at him. "You want to buy the worst-looking tree on the lot?"

Something in her voice sounded odd, but he just shrugged. "Sure. I know it seems lame, but I figure even sad trees need a home. But it needs planting after Christmas, so if you wouldn't mind having another tree in your yard, I'll buy it. I can't take it back to Dallas with me. Even if I could, I don't have a yard."

Chloe nodded slowly, her gaze direct and unwavering. "You are welcome to plant the tree in my yard."

Then saying nothing else, she crossed the small distance between them and kissed him.

CHAPTER 7

CHLOE HADN'T INTENDED on kissing Evan.

Not at all.

In fact, it was the last thing she'd ever planned on doing. But when he'd made that statement about the sad tree needing a home, she couldn't resist.

One thing that had made her father such a sincere, admirable man had been his empathy for others, including small, lonely trees.

To find that same level of empathy in Evan was overwhelming. Who would expect a successful corporate attorney to have a tender heart? Especially one who worked for Peter Thomas.

Still, she probably should have given him a little warning about the kiss. Not that he was complaining.

His arm went around her waist, and his lips

parted, and the next thing she knew they were in a deep passionate kiss that curled her toes.

Oh, my goodness! What had she started? Chloe leaned against him, inhaling his masculine scent and the aroma of pine trees, and sighed a deep sigh of satisfaction.

He tightened his grip, and she made a soft little noise of approval, encouraging him to keep up what he was doing. They kept kissing and kissing and kissing, caught up in the beautiful moment, hidden from view by the Christmas trees.

Finally, they had to come up for air, and Evan loosened his grip on her a little.

"Um, I guess I should say I'm sorry," she whispered, although she wasn't at all. "Kissing you out of the blue like that."

He smiled slowly and told her, "I'm not sorry, and you shouldn't be either."

Shyly, she returned his smile. "Good. Me neither."

Evan took a step closer, and she was fairly certain he planned on kissing her again...

"I found it!" Peter shouted from somewhere deep in the pine tree thicket.

"So much for that," Chloe murmured.

"Let's talk later." His eyes lowered, and the look he gave her was so sexy that Chloe had to remind herself to take a breath.

She nodded and tried to get her runaway pulse under control. "Yes, let's do."

"For now, we better go find out what Peter found." His smile sent a tingle jumping along her nerve endings.

"Uh-huh, I'm dying to see just how big this tree is."

He inclined his head and swept out his arm for her to go ahead of him as if she were royalty. Chloe simply couldn't help herself. She giggled like a schoolgirl with a mad crush.

"Evan!" Peter bellowed. "Where are you?"

They followed the sound of Peter's voice and found him standing with Ruby next to a King Kong-sized tree.

Peter's face was lit up like the Las Vegas strip. He walked around the tree, hands clasped behind his back, eying the pine from the tip-top branch to the base of the trunk.

Her mother, however, looked appalled. "This thing is *huge*."

"I know." Peter gleefully rubbed his palms together.

Ruby stretched her head as far back as it would go, sizing up the massive tree. "I think it's for businesses."

"Exactly."

"I'm not even sure it will fit in the house you are

renting. The ceilings are high, but not high enough for this tree. It's got to be twenty feet tall."

"Nonsense." Peter laughed. "Sure, it'll fit. It's just a tree." He turned and looked at Evan. "Go pay for this and schedule it for delivery."

Evan looked at his boss for a long minute, then looked at the tree. He opened his mouth, then closed it. Chloe could tell that he wanted to argue, but he didn't.

"Fine," Evan said, an exasperated expression crossing his face. "But for the record, I agree with Ruby. This tree looks too big for the house."

"Bigger is *always* better," Peter said, sounding like a petulant thirteen-year-old. "When you pay for the tree, ask them if anyone around here offers tree decorating service. There's got to be someone who decorates trees for old people or the infirm."

There were a few people Chloe could recommend for the chore, but she was reluctant to provide Peter with that information.

"And whoever you find," Peter went on. "Make sure they know this tree needs that *wow* factor. I want jaws to drop and eyes to go wide. If you can't find anyone in this one-horse town, call up my people in Dallas and get them out here ASAP."

Evan scowled, pulled up the collar of his coat against the sudden gust of wind, flattened his lips, and shook his head. "Fine," he said, the word coming out brittle as flint.

Chloe tried to think of something to say that wouldn't sound judgmental, but she couldn't think of a thing. She hadn't been lying when she'd said she believed people should have the tree that brought them joy, and Peter clearly looked joyful. But it was the joy of showing off, not the joy for the tree itself.

"Why is it so important to knock the socks off people with a tree?" she asked, knowing she should drop it. "I thought the point of this party was to make amends to the people of Kringle."

Ruby shot her an expression that said *keep your opinions to yourself, sweetheart.*

But Chloe couldn't help herself. "I thought you wanted to be like Scrooge after the ghosts. After the ghosts visit him, Scrooge is generous and kind."

Peter laughed and shot her mother a glance. "Your girl is naïve, Ruby."

"Thank you, Peter," her mother said calmly.

Peter's eyebrows shot up on his forehead. "I didn't mean that as a compliment."

"If by naïve you mean my daughter is considerate and humble, I don't see any other way to take it than a compliment."

Peter seemed flabbergasted. "I'm no Scrooge."

Ruby cleared her throat.

"Scrooge was stingy," Peter said. "*I am* generous. Look at the party I'm throwing for the entire town. Look at the size of this tree. Do you have any idea how much money this shindig is costing me?"

Chloe couldn't believe what he was saying. "You almost killed Kringle when you convinced the Madisons to move their candy factory to Dallas."

"That's not on me. That's on the town for putting all their eggs in one basket." Peter snorted.

Anger pulsed through her, and Chloe's mouth fell open. "Y-you didn't even care what you did to our town."

Peter's eyes met Ruby's, and he shook his head again. "Naïve as the day is long." To Chloe he said, "Business is business. If I considered how every business transaction that I make would harm everyone involved, I'd be as broke as the rest of the people around here."

Yes, okay, maybe businesses couldn't always make smart financial decisions that also took individual needs into account, but the impact of Peter's maneuvering had been as huge as that pine tree he wanted stuffed into his house.

Gritting her teeth, Chloe ground out, "And what about my mother?"

Ruby moved toward her. "Chloe, Peter apologized, and I accepted his apology. This is between the two of us."

"You don't even care that he left you at the—"

"It was better that we didn't get married," Peter said. "It wouldn't have worked. Our values are just too different. I'm big city, and she's small-town country all the way."

Dear heavens, this guy was a total jerk.

Several rude responses occurred to Chloe, but the look her mother gave her made it clear she wanted her to drop the subject. Chloe loved and respected her mother, and she knew that Ruby was more than capable of standing up for herself. She didn't need—and didn't want—Chloe to do it for her.

Fine, she thought, echoing what Evan had said before he went off to pay for the tree. It was none of her business. Her mother could handle her own affairs.

Hurt and angry, Chloe turned and headed toward the front of the tree lot, putting as much distance between herself and Peter as possible.

Once she was out of view of her mother and Peter, Chloe stopped and took several long deep breaths, struggling to get herself under control. The air was ripe with the scent of pine trees, and for a moment, she simply enjoyed the smell. She had to be around Peter without getting so upset. She was letting him ruin her Christmas, and if she were honest, he wasn't a danger to her or her mother.

Why was she being so reactive?

Her mother was a smart cookie, and it was clear she wasn't falling for Peter again. No one in town believed his hooey anymore, so they expected nothing from him. She had to face facts. If she wanted Peter's perfect Christmas not to ruin *her* perfect Christmas, she needed to ignore him.

She found Evan at the front of the Christmas tree lot. He stood next to a small wooden table containing a cash box. Two teens, who'd just put money inside the cash box, were talking to Evan.

"Hey," she called out, and that breathless feeling she experienced whenever she was around Evan came over her again.

Evan turned and smiled at her. "Hi there."

As usual, his smile made her heart race, and she grinned in return.

Beside him stood that scraggly little tree he'd picked out.

"You really bought the runt," she said.

"Of course. And a deal is a deal. You already agreed to let me plant it in your yard. You can't change your mind now."

She had no intention of changing her mind. "A promise is a promise." She chuckled. "I'll also help you decorate it."

Evan picked up the tree and headed toward the car. "You say that as if you had a choice in the matter. I always expected you to help with the decorating."

Chloe laughed at his silliness, happy to have shifted off the grim mood she'd developed after talking with Peter.

"I must drop by the store and get some decorations," he said, picking up the Charlie Brown tree.

Memories of her childhood flooded back to her. Memories of her dad buying just such a tree. Her heart squeezed, feeling a little lopsided with nostalgia and a strange kind of unexpected joy. "I have lots of decorations at my house. No need to buy more."

"That's generous, but what about your own tree?" he asked, walking toward his SUV. The tree was so small he carried it easily in his arms.

She went ahead of him to open the back of the vehicle and then stepped back so he could angle the tree inside.

"Did you already decorate your tree and you've got leftover decorations?" he asked.

"I put up a tree at my clinic each year. Since I spend Christmas at my mom's, I rarely have one at my house. I just help Mom with hers."

Except she *hadn't* helped this year. She'd been so busy with work that she hadn't been able to find time to help. But Peter had.

Now, considering his current behavior, Chloe had to wonder why he'd been so helpful.

She'd thought he was being nice, but now she wasn't so sure. His motivation for helping with her mother's tree had probably been self-serving. More and more of his actions looked like they were.

While they waited for Ruby and Peter, they both leaned against the SUV. Chloe sent her mother a quick text. She waited two minutes, but Ruby didn't answer.

Chloe eyed the phone. "I'm not sure what's taking them so long."

"I'm sure they'll be along soon," he said. "Unless..." He got a funny look on his face.

When his words drifted off, Chloe turned toward him. "No way."

"I said nothing," he pointed out.

"You don't need to. You thought that maybe they are kissing, but they aren't." Just the thought of it upset her. Surely her mother could see through Peter's act and she wasn't canoodling with the man.

Evan shrugged. "Well, you know, this Christmas tree lot seems to inspire ideas."

Chloe could hardly argue since she'd kissed him not ten minutes ago. "That was different."

He shot her a questioning look.

"I kissed you because you'd done something nice."

"Ah. And you have doubts that Peter can do something nice, right?"

"Not nice enough to deserve a kiss."

"Maybe they're fighting. Would that make more sense?"

He might be onto something. Peter sure had gotten on Chloe's unpleasant side tonight. Maybe her mother had lost patience with him as well.

Just then Ruby and Peter walked out of the tree lot. Her mother didn't seem the least bit agitated, and Chloe relaxed a little. From that total lack of tension between Peter and her mother, Chloe was pretty sure they hadn't been kissing or fighting.

"They will deliver the tree tomorrow morning," Evan told Peter. "And the guy who owns this tree lot could find a company to decorate it. They'll be by in the afternoon."

Without even saying "thank you," Peter climbed in the front passenger seat and shut the door.

Evan winced and shook his head, then moved to open the back door for Chloe and her mother to slide inside. He shut the door, got behind the wheel, and started the engine.

Ruby said, "Peter, you wanted to say something to Evan, right?"

Curious, Chloe glanced at her mother, but Ruby was staring at the back of Peter's head as if she could drill common decency into him with just a look.

"Um...er..." Peter mumbled. "Thank you for your help, Evan."

Chloe shot a smile at her mom, who smiled back. Ha! She should have known her mom would whip Peter Thomas into shape.

* * *

Standing in the living room of Chloe's cute little bungalow, Evan tipped his head and studied the tree. The thin branches could hardly hold the lightest of ornaments. Decorating it with traditional balls and trinkets was out of the question. As soon as he hung a large red glass ball on the tree, it leaned.

"It's too spindly for decorations." Evan sighed.

"Poor little thing." She removed the glass ball, and the tree straightened immediately, and she could have sworn it looked relieved. "Maybe we could make a garland out of construction paper? That should be light enough."

"Great idea." Evan chuckled. He was glad to see Chloe looking relaxed and happy after the day they'd had with his boss.

He knew that Peter annoyed her, so he was really glad that his boss had called it an early night and asked Evan to drop him off at the rental house. They took Ruby home first, then when they swung by the rental property to let Peter out, he and Chloe stopped long enough to check on Vixen.

They'd gotten pizza and brought it back to her place and ate it curled up on the couch by the fire before tackling the tree. He perched on the edge of the fireplace hearth, the warm heat at his back from the gas fire, and tilted his head to consider the sad sack tree.

Immediately, Chloe's fluffy white dog hopped on his lap.

"I don't believe it." Chloe laughed. "First the tree and now Snowball."

Huh? Confused, he straightened his chin and met her steady gaze. "What are you talking about it?"

She sat next to him on the hearth. "My dog likes you."

"Is that monumental?"

"Oh, very. Snowball doesn't like people," she said. "Especially men. She hates them. As long as I've known her, she'd let no men touch her. And even with women, she takes forever to warm up to strangers. She just hopped right into your lap."

"She's a sweetie. I'm really starting to like dogs." Evan glanced at the animal snuggled in his lap and scratched behind her ears. "She seems happy now."

"She likes you." Chloe flashed a grin at him.

They exchanged glances. A beat passed.

Audibly, Chloe sucked in her breath and said, "I like you, too."

Evan didn't hesitate. "Ditto."

They grinned at each other.

He leaned over to kiss Chloe, but Snowball started barking.

Evan pulled back.

Snowball stopped barking and settled into his lap once more.

He leaned in again, lips pursed.

Snowball growled.

He eased away from Chloe.

Snowball thumped her tail.

Evan and Chloe both stared at the dog, then at each other, and burst out laughing.

"Um…" Evan said. "I hate to break it to you, but I think your dog is jealous."

Chloe laughed again, a light, carefree sound. Evan quickly joined in.

"How odd. She's never acted this way before. In fact, my mom is the only other person she likes. She tolerates a few other females, but you really are the first male she's bonded with."

Evan petted Snowball. "I'm flattered."

"You should be."

Just to test the theory, Evan leaned toward Chloe again, and Snowball barked at Chloe.

"Oh, my goodness," Chloe said. "She *is* jealous."

"Some people have got it," Evan teased. "And some don't."

"Downshift the ego, buddy." Chloe giggled. "We have another problem."

"What's that?"

"The tree. Poor thing looks too skimpy all naked there."

At the word "naked," Evan felt his entire body light up, and an image so provocative popped into his mind. An image involving Chloe and a lack of clothing.

"We should get on that construction paper garland," she murmured, her gaze fixed on his mouth.

"We could make snowflakes from computer paper too," he suggested. "It'll be fun."

"I'll go get my laptop and look up images." She

hopped up from the hearth and headed to her bedroom.

For the next half hour, they printed paper ornaments and cut them out, adding them to the tree one by one. After they added just a few scattered snowflakes and the construction paper garland, the tree listed to one side again.

"This is one wimpy tree," Evan moved some ornaments around to even out the weight and straightened the tree once more. "We're already maxed out on decorations."

Smiling, Chloe circled the tree. She seemed unconcerned about the tree's inability to take on more ornaments. "The tree has heart. That's what really matters."

He liked the way she thought.

Deciding that they'd done all they could do, they moved the doggy gate so Snowball wouldn't be able to get at the tree, and then they watered it.

"Well, Snowball, now you have some company," Chloe said.

Snowball seemed to approve of the tree. She ran over to the gate and peered at the small pine through the bars. She did a little merry dance, wriggling her tail and turning in a circle, and looked up at Evan with expectation.

"What is it, girl?" he asked, bending at the waist and resting his palms on his upper thighs.

She barked and wagged her tail harder.

"Um, does she need something?" He glanced up at Chloe.

"She wants to go for a walk," Chloe explained. "She must think you're the kind of fella who's up for a moonlight stroll."

Evan chuckled. "Sure, I'm game. Where's her leash?"

Chloe got the leash, and they put on their coats, then headed out the door.

"Which way?" Evan asked once they were on the sidewalk.

"Let's wander downtown," she said. "And see the lights."

"Sounds like a plan."

The air was crisp but not too cold. Almost all the houses were decorated with lights and lawn orna-ments. The smell of Christmas floated on the air—pine, cinnamon, gingerbread. In the distance they heard Christmas music. When they got to the town square, they spied a group of carolers standing on the street corner singing, "I'll be Home for Christmas."

"Looks like the high school choir is serenading tourists," Chloe said.

They headed toward the music. Teens in bright-red and green sweaters, their clear youthful voices lifted high, walked from the street corner to the front steps of the town hall, people following them.

They joined the crowd encircling the singers.

Snowball yipped and tugged on her leash, eager to be part of the festivities.

Evan picked her up and held the small dog close to his chest while he and Chloe listened to the music. When the short concert finished, they strolled toward Chloe's clinic.

"Do you mind if I stop in and see my overnight patients?" she asked.

"Of course not."

They went inside, and Evan waited in the lobby with Snowball while Chloe headed to the back to check in with the overnight vet tech. She came out a few minutes later, and they continued their walk in the opposite direction, away from the town square.

"So," Chloe said after they walked in companionable silence for several minutes. "What are your Christmas Day plans? Are you and Peter staying in Kringle for the holiday itself, or will you head home after his Christmas Eve party?"

Evan angled her a sideways glance. "Honestly, I haven't thought about it."

"No plans to spend it with your family?"

"My parents live in Boston near my sister. Since Peter ordered me to come here and help him with the party..." Evan shrugged. "I'd planned on flying up for New Year's instead."

"I see."

But from the look on her face, he could tell she didn't understand at all. "My family..." He paused, weighing out his words. "We're all high achievers. It's common for us to put work ahead of other things."

"Like spending the holidays with each other?"

He nodded, suddenly feeling extraordinarily lonely for no reason he could figure out.

"Your job means a lot to you then." She had her head down and her arms wrapped around her.

"I..." Honestly, he had no idea how to answer that.

"You value monetary success over personal relationships." Now it was her turn to pause before she added, "Like Peter."

"No!" he said more sharply than he intended. "Not like Peter. Not like Peter at *all*."

"Good," she said, a faint smile flitting across her mouth as she raised her eyes to meet his. "I'm glad."

The smile did strange and lovely things to him. It made him want...

Well, what *did* he want?

He looked into her face and felt all kinds of emotions he hadn't expected to feel. Longing, acute loneliness, and a powerful desire to kiss her all over again. Her hair fell across her forehead in an adorable sweep, bringing an extra softness to her features. Then she gave him a look so gentle it felt like a caress.

"Do you ever think about leaving Peter's firm?" she asked, skirting around a pile of leaves the wind had blown into a heap on the sidewalk. "Or do you think he'll make you partner one day?"

Hmm, why was she asking? As an attorney, he looked for hidden motives in people, but Chloe's expression was guileless.

Until this Christmas, he'd thought he wanted to become a partner in Peter's firm. But now? After seeing his boss' behavior in Kringle, after meeting Chloe, his ambitions had shifted. Did he really want to continue his association with Peter?

Why *not* start his own firm?

"Do you really like working for Peter?"

"Honestly," he said. "Like has never really figured into it. I'm good at what I do. I enjoy making sense of the legal system—"

"But are you happy?"

He stopped.

So did she.

Snowball sank down on her haunches at their feet.

Their eyes met.

He studied Chloe. He knew she didn't like Peter, and probably she wanted to hear him say he was considering branching out on his own, but he saw no judgment in her eyes. Just simple curiosity.

"I don't think I can answer that question," he murmured.

She nodded, and the saddest expression came over her. "That's what I thought."

Suddenly, Evan felt as if he'd lost something very important to him that he'd never even known he possessed.

She dropped her gaze and started walking again. Away from the town square, they could see more of the starry night sky. They walked in silence, their footsteps crunching against the fallen leaves. The air rich with the aroma of many suppers being cooked in the neighborhood they passed through.

Evan stopped walking again and leaned his head back to stare at the sky. "The number of stars you can see here is amazing. In Dallas, I'm lucky if I can spot Orion and his belt during the fall and winter."

"You know the stars?"

"Yep." He chuckled. "Deep down I'm a science nerd, particularly astronomy."

"Oh, fun." Chloe tilted her head back too. "Show Orion to me. I know nothing about stars or constellations."

Since the sky in Kringle was significantly clearer than in Dallas, Evan had no problem finding the correct stars, and he pointed upward. "It's easy to spot Orion's belt this time of year. The stars line up nicely."

Chloe stood for a moment, gazing at the sky, and then she shifted her attention to him. "Amazing, but you better not tell Abby Owens that the stars are in a line. She sure got after you about those dalmatian spots."

Evan burst out laughing. "Good point."

They'd reached the end of the block. Chloe waved, indicating that they should cross the street and head back toward her house.

In the darkness, Evan spied the silhouette of a building that looked a bit out of place in the neighborhood. It was only partially visible above the roofline of the houses, but its dark shape was hard to miss. The structure looked sad and forgotten.

"What's that building?" he asked.

Chloe tipped her head to see where he was pointing. "Oh, that was the headquarters for Kringle Kandy. The Madisons have tried several times to sell the building, but they've had no luck. Same with their house you're renting. No one seems to want to buy them."

Evan could understand why. Neither the house nor the factory fit in with the rest of the town.

Just as they reached Chloe's house, his cell phone buzzed in his pocket. He handed Snowball's leash to Chloe and glanced at the phone. It was Peter.

Evan answered. "Yes?"

"Come here," Peter commanded. "Right now. I need you. Something's wrong."

CHAPTER 8

CHLOE GLANCED at the emergency room clock. Ten p.m.

Three hours. It had been three hours since Evan called the ambulance and they rushed Peter to the hospital.

At the moment, she, Evan, and Ruby were all sitting in the emergency department waiting area.

So far, the only information they had gotten about Peter was that it didn't seem to be another heart attack. Once the tests came back, the doctor would know more.

Chloe wanted to say something encouraging or helpful to Evan and her mother, but she had no idea what to say. When she and Evan had gotten to the house, they'd found Peter in the study, sitting on the floor, his face pale, sweat beading his brow, and his hand clasped to his chest.

Immediately, they called 9-1-1.

"It's that dog's fault," Peter had kept muttering.

Leaving Evan with Peter, Chloe went over to see what was going on with Vixen. On the surface, the dog and her puppies seemed fine, although Vixen was cowering and curled protectively around her babies she'd herded into a huddle.

When she saw Chloe, Vixen wagged her tail and edged from the corner toward the center of the makeshift bed.

Chloe patted the dog, then went back to Evan and Peter.

"The Hutchison deal fell through," Peter was saying through clenched teeth.

"What do you mean? It's Saturday. Why are you doing business on a Saturday?"

"I hadn't heard from Hutchison. He missed the deadline, so I called him." Peter mopped his brow with the back of his hand.

"You were supposed to be taking a vacation," Evan chided, perching on the arm of the couch next to where his boss was sitting. If you needed something done, you should have asked me to handle it. That's what I'm here for. To make things easier on you."

Peter made a scoffing noise. "This is *my* business. It's not something you could have handled."

Evan shifted his gaze to Chloe. "How's Vixen?"

"Who cares about that damn dog?" Peter growled. "I'm the one in pain."

"We've called 9-1-1," Evan assured him. "They're on the way. Try not to get upset. It's important that you stay calm."

"You want me calm? Then move that mutt out of here." Peter's eyes narrowed, his palm still splayed across his chest. "I was trying to take care of business, and just because I might have raised my voice a bit, that mongrel started barking. I told her to shut up, but she wouldn't stop."

Chloe froze, anger pushing through her hot as lava. No wonder Vixen had been sheltering her pups and cowering in the corner. Chloe wanted to tell Peter off, but now wasn't the time. They were both upset, and he could very well be in the throes of a second heart attack.

The ambulance arrived, and once the paramedics took over, Evan and Chloe got out of the way and let them do their jobs. They swung by to pick up Ruby and the three of them drove to the hospital to wait on news of Peter's condition.

Chloe glanced over at Evan, who was sitting next to her in the waiting room. She felt bad for him. Peter had put Evan in an awkward situation.

On the drive to Ruby's house, Evan had apologized for Peter's attitude toward Vixen, and she could tell his boss' behavior upset him, but his hands were pretty well tied. He worked for Peter. If he valued his job, he had to hold his tongue. Especially with someone as unpredictable as Peter Thomas.

She understood that, but she couldn't square away the disappointment she felt in Evan.

A middle-aged woman wearing a lab jacket, her hair piled on top of her head in a tight bun, came through the double doors that led back to the emergency bays. Embroidered across the pocket of her lab jacket was the title, *Dr. Worthington.* "Who's with Peter Thomas?"

Evan stood up. "We are."

Chloe rose to her feet, joining him. She wanted Evan to know he wasn't alone. Her mother got up too.

"How is he?" Evan asked.

"He's fine," Dr. Worthington said. "It wasn't a cardiac event."

"What happened?" Evan shifted his weight.

"Most likely, an anxiety attack. To be on the safe side, though, his cardiologist in Dallas has asked that we keep him overnight and monitor him. One of you can go talk to him if you'd like."

That was good news.

Ruby looked relieved and let out a little sigh. Chloe wrapped her arm around her mother's shoulders and gave her a little squeeze.

"You go," Chloe said to Evan. "We'll wait here."

Evan nodded and followed Dr. Worthington through the double doors.

Once Evan had gone, they sat back down, and Chloe told her mother the details of what had happened, including what Peter had said about Vixen.

Looking concerned, her mother worried the strap of her purse with her fingers. "Do you think Peter hurt the dog or her puppies?"

Chloe shook her head. "No. Not physically at least. But he yelled at Vixen, and the poor thing seemed terrified. I'll move them to the clinic in the morning since Peter is staying here overnight. Then after work, I'll take them to my house, but I'm not sure it's wise for Snowball to be around the puppies at the moment. She's rambunctious, and the puppies are still so tiny. Can Snowball stay with you?"

"Of course." Her mother gnawed her bottom lip and glanced around the waiting room.

Chloe knew being here at the hospital was tough on her. They'd sat in this very waiting area when they'd brought her father to the hospital that very last time. They'd even talked before about how hospitals unsettled Ruby. It had been very brave of her to come here for Peter. She hoped the man appreciated how much it had taken out of Ruby to be here, but she doubted it.

"You can head on home, Mom. I'll call you a ride," Chloe offered.

"No. I'll wait for Evan. I'm fine." She reached over to pat Chloe's hand. "Honestly."

For a few minutes, they sat in silence, then her mother softly said, "You know, I don't like him very much."

Chloe glanced at her mother, unsure that she'd heard her correctly. "Evan?"

"Oh, heavens no. I adore Evan. I don't like Peter. There. I've said it. I don't wish him any harm, and I'm very glad that he's going to be okay, but I don't like him, and I have no idea why I ever thought I wanted to marry that man."

"Huh?" Gobsmacked, Chloe could only stare. She'd never once heard her generous mother openly admit to not liking someone. Over the years, there had been a few occasions when Chloe had suspected that her mother might not be too fond of a person, but Ruby had never come right out and said such a thing.

Until tonight.

Not really certain what to say, Chloe raised her eyebrows and ventured, "I don't like him either."

"There's one thing I keep asking myself," Mom said.

"What's that?"

"Why is someone with so much integrity as Evan working for a man like Peter?"

Hmm, Chloe thought. That was the sixty-four-thousand-dollar question, wasn't it?

* * *

After leaving Peter in the hospital, Evan had taken Ruby and Chloe home, then gone back to the house to look after Vixen and her puppies. Later, he'd fallen into a restless sleep where he wrestled with his conscience and his future both in and out of his dreams. The next morning, right after breakfast, Chloe dropped by to pick up the dog and her babies.

"I'm taking them to the clinic for now," she said. "Would you like to come along? Afterward we could go to the Kringle Village, just for a little R&R after last night's episode. You need a break."

Evan had said "yes" without thinking twice, but now that he was here at Kringle Village, he was having second thoughts.

He stood at the top of the man-made hill and watched as a teenaged boy with spiky green hair and a wild laugh slid down it on a giant candy-cane-striped inner tube.

"What's this again?" he asked Chloe, staring at an identical inner tube the attendant handed him.

She laughed, looking oh-so-comfy and cute in a fluffy red sweater, a blue jean jacket, and yoga pants, sitting on a tube of her own next to where he was standing.

"It's snow tubing," she explained. "Sit down and strap yourself in for a fun ride. You're going to love it."

Evan wasn't so sure, but hey, he'd give it a shot.

He'd promised Chloe he'd try to enjoy himself. Gingerly, he eased down onto the inner tube.

Laughing, Chloe shoved off and started bouncing down the hill in the lane next to his and called out over her shoulder, "Last one to the bottom is a rotten egg."

With a push, he headed down his own lane, bouncing and swerving as he went. His pulse quickened with the same thrill he used to get as a kid on those rare trips where his parents took them to an amusement park.

The bottom seemed so far away.

To his left and several yards ahead of him on the downhill slope, Chloe was hanging on tight to her inner tube and hollering, "Woo-hoo!"

Man, but he loved her zest for life. She made every little thing feel like a grand adventure.

He had to admit, this was fun. *She* was fun.

By the time he reached the bottom of the hill, his pulse was going lickety-split, and he was breathing fast, and his whole body felt free in a way it hadn't in a very long time. Dang, he was sorry the ride over.

At the bottom of the hill, Chloe was waiting for him, bouncing up and down on the balls of her feet. "Isn't it fun?"

He nodded. "Yes. I can see why you like it."

"Come on, let's go again," she said and grabbed his hand.

He didn't argue. And for the next half hour, they

enjoyed going up the stairs and then sliding down the hill again. Even though Kringle Village was crowded on a Sunday, the lines moved quickly, and they made several more runs before calling it quits for lunch.

Although it had been cold inside the snow tubing building, the weather outside was in the low fifties. The forecast said they expected colder weather in the next couple of days, but at the moment, it was nice outside in the sunshine. They grabbed salads from a food court restaurant and then located a free round table.

"I'm having the best time," Evan admitted, spearing a tomato with a plastic fork. "You're right. I needed to break loose and have some fun. Especially after last night."

Chloe's look was downright smug. "Told you so."

Evan's phone dinged, and he pulled it from his pocket, then sighed.

"What it is?" Chloe asked.

"Peter's being discharged." Evan suppressed a sigh. "He's ready for me to pick him up."

"Well," Chloe said. "At least you got a few hours of reprieve."

"There is that." He chuckled, trying not to view fetching his boss as a burden. He dabbed his mouth with a napkin. "I suppose I should get on over there."

"I'll come with you."

"You don't have to do that."

Chloe caught his eye. "I *want* to be with you."

His heart knocked against his chest. He wanted to be with her too. Slowly, he nodded. "I'd like the company."

She reached across the table and squeezed his hand, and for the first time in a long time, Evan didn't feel so alone.

The phone dinged again. Peter texting in all caps. COME GET ME.

This time, Evan couldn't hold back the sigh. He pushed back his chair, and Chloe followed suit. They bussed their table and were heading for the door when a tall, gangly man that Evan recognized came up to them.

His name was Rich Honeycutt, and he was the elder of Kringle Kakes. Evan remembered meeting him and his wife when he and Peter had bought that sheet cake for the Christmas Eve party that was roughly the size of Rhode Island.

"Hello," Evan greeted him.

"Tell your boss to stop texting me," Rich said, looking harried and irritated.

"What?" Evan blinked.

"We're not interested in moving our business to Dallas."

Evan shook his head. "Peter's been trying to get you to move your business?"

"Yes." Rich hardened his jaw. "And not just Kringle Kakes either. He's approached the owners of

Kringle Village and Kringle Kafe as well. Apparently, he's buying a strip mall in Dallas and is looking for businesses from Kringle that he can convince to move there."

Evan felt his jaw drop. "You've got to be kidding me."

Rich grimaced. "I wish I was. And he's making some wild promises." Rich told him how Peter was making pie-in-the-sky projections about franchising the business.

Evan peered over at Chloe. She didn't seem surprised.

"I knew he was up to something underhanded," she muttered. "I didn't want to believe it, so I gave him the benefit of the doubt."

"Ah," Evan said as the puzzle pieces fell into place. "I think I know why he had a panic attack last night."

Chloe canted her head. "Why is that?"

"Remember the Hutchinson deal he was talking about that fell through?"

"Yes."

"It was the strip mall."

"Well, maybe it's all for the best that the deal fell through." Chloe sank her hands on her hips.

"Yeah," Rich Honeycutt said. "Especially since none of us intended on selling to him. Maybe he'll stop texting me now."

"Thanks for letting me know," Evan told Honeycutt. "I'll make sure he gets the message that you aren't interested in hearing from him further."

"I appreciate it." Rich nodded and headed out the door.

Leaving Evan and Chloe staring at each other.

"I know he's your boss," Chloe said. "But I disapprove of Peter's behavior."

Me too, Evan thought. *Me too.*

And just like that, all the tossing and turning he'd done the night before coalesced into a firm decision. "I'm going to resign today."

"What?" Chloe blinked. She looked surprised but pleased. "Really? Are you sure? I know you've worked hard to get where you are. You shouldn't do something rash."

He shook his head, certain that this was the right choice. "I'm not being rash. It's been eating at the back of my mind for a while, although I didn't fully realize it until I came to Kringle and saw how he's acted."

"But how will you make a living?"

"I have a good reputation as a lawyer, and finding another job at another corporate law firm shouldn't be an issue, *if* that's what I decide I want."

"If?"

"I'm not sure what I want except that I no longer wish to work for Peter. I don't approve of how he conducts business and how he treats people, and I don't want to be associated with him anymore."

Chloe gave him a sweet smile, then went up on tiptoes and planted a soft kiss on his cheek.

"You are an extraordinary man, Evan Conner," she whispered.

And in that moment, he felt like the king of the world.

* * *

Evan took Chloe home and went to pick up Peter. His boss spent the entire drive back to the rental house grousing about how awful his care had been and how glad he was to get out of that hicktown hospital—to use his words.

He waited until they'd gotten into the house and Peter settled on the couch before he broke the news that he was resigning. "I'll have my resignation letter to you by tomorrow morning. I'll finish up the current cases I'm working on, but after the first of the year, I am gone."

Peter scowled. "You can't just quit out of the blue."

"But I am."

His boss' eyes narrowed, and Evan could see his mental machinations as he searched for a way to manipulate Evan.

"The firm counts on you," Peter said.

"You'll hire someone to take my place," Evan said calmly, reasonably.

"But you're special." Peter leveled him a winsome look. "You get me like no one else."

"Exactly," Evan said. "Which is why I'm leaving."

Just that quick, Peter's mood changed. His smile disappeared, and he hopped to his feet, snarling. "I can ruin you."

"You forget, I know where the bodies are buried." Evan used the figure of speech, referring to some of Peter's shadier business dealings. He hoped he was looking a lot calmer than he felt. Inside, he was shaking like a leaf, but he couldn't afford to let Peter view him as weak. "I can ruin you just as swiftly as you can ruin me. It's in your best interest to let me go without a fight."

"You're making too big of a deal out of this," Peter said, back to wheedling. He waved a dismissive hand. "So what if I tried to make a few bucks by getting some of the local businesses to move to Dallas? Big deal."

"You don't consider people's livelihoods a big deal?"

"Pfftt." Peter waved a hand over his head. "They'll do way better business in Dallas than they do here."

"That's not universally true. You know as well as I do that many of those businesses only thrive because they are in Kringle. If you move Kringle Kakes to a strip mall in Dallas, it's just one more bakery, and odds are it won't make it. But here in Kringle, it's the only bakery. It's a bakery that specializes in Christmas treats in a town that's known for Christmas."

"I didn't make any promises," Peter said. "They know the risks."

"Yes, you made promises," Evan reminded him. "Rich Honeycutt said you promised he'd be able to expand and even branch off into franchises in a few years, but you know that his chances of that happening are almost nonexistent. I've looked at the numbers. The bakery would be doomed if it moved."

Peter shrugged. "Since when do you care about a bunch of local yokels? So what if Honeycutt failed? All I needed to do was guarantee that I could fill the strip mall."

Lots of responses occurred to Evan, many of them including curse words, but he let it go. He didn't feel like fighting with Peter. He had his own life to focus on, a life that for the first time in years excited him.

"I'm staying in Kringle until after Christmas," he said. "So, I'll be here for your party. After that, I'm gone."

He headed toward the door, turning at the last moment to add a final thought. "You know, Peter, you and I could both learn something important from the people in this town. Life shouldn't be just about deals and money. Love and happiness are a lot more important."

And with that, he left the room before he could

hear whatever snarky comment was on the tip of Peter's tongue. He'd heard enough from his soon-to-be ex-boss over the last few days to last him a lifetime. He no longer wanted to hear anymore from him.

He had plans to make.

CHAPTER 9

IT WAS CHRISTMAS EVE, and Peter's party was in full swing.

Chloe glanced around the foyer of the Madison house. The place looked terrific. Rather than hiring a fancy big city firm to handle the decorations and catering, Evan had hired the Kringle Kafe owners, Sandy and Walter Hughes.

Sandy told her this morning that they hadn't even considered expanding their business into catering until Evan had explained how they could grow their income through it. They'd ended up hiring on three part-time employees to help with the catering tonight, and they hope to add catering as a service option permanently.

"The place looks amazing," her mother said, coming to stand next to Chloe. "Sandy and Walter have a real flare for decorating, and the food is so yummy. Did you try the rumaki?" Ruby kissed her fingertips. "To die for. I'm so glad Evan hired someone local."

Chloe was happy about that too. She'd heard through the grapevine that Peter had returned to Dallas and Evan was now in charge of the party. Supposedly, Peter was ticked off at Evan for resigning, so he'd hired a town car service to drive out from Dallas to pick him up.

Chloe was glad Evan had quit. No matter what he did, he deserved much better than a life of constant work that he'd had with Peter.

Happy that Peter was out of all their lives, Chloe followed her mother through the crowded living room to the dining area. Here the Hughes had done another great job decorating with snowflakes and tinsel theme.

As they'd feared when Peter bought it, the Christmas tree had proven too big to move inside the house, so it was now standing in the middle of the backyard looking more than a little ridiculous. The company Evan had located had done a marvellous job decorating it, but Chloe still preferred the sweet little tree they'd set up at her house.

"I hear Evan is asking around about planting the tree after the party," Ruby said.

It stunned Chloe. "I didn't know that."

Ruby nodded. "I don't think he wanted to tell

you until he was certain, but apparently if done right, some Christmas trees can."

He impressed Chloe. Evan had been busy during the last couple of days.

Her mother moved farther into the house, and Chloe followed. From the family room, she heard beautiful voices singing.

"He hired a choir?" she asked.

Ruby nodded. "I heard from Jolie Stuart that Evan hired the high school choir to sing. He's paying them enough that they can afford their spring trip to Galveston. I know I keep saying it, but that's only because it's true. Evan Conner is a really nice man, and I'm glad he came to Kringle."

"Really? He did all that?"

Ruby nodded.

"I'd like to thank him for being so kind."

"There he is. Go tell him." Ruby nodded.

Evan had come through the door, a stack of firewood in his arms and a dusting of snow in his hair. His head was thrown back, and he was laughing at something Rich Honeycutt had said. Rich had come in behind him, also carrying firewood.

In that instant, Evan's eyes caught her gaze and held it.

Chloe's heart jumped into her throat, and she froze, overcome with an overwhelming emotion. For just a heartbeat, she stood still, trying to make sense of what she was feeling.

He deposited the firewood on the hearth, dusted himself off, and turned to her, a twinkle in his dark eyes.

Her breath stilled.

Then she knew what she was feeling. She was falling in love. The sensation washed over her like a warm summer sunshine.

He was the kindest man she'd ever met other than her father. He was an exceptional person who accepted responsibility and tried his best to be honest, and she couldn't wait to get to know him better.

Despite everything that had happened with Peter, he had stayed in town and made sure the party was a hit because the people of Kringle were expecting a celebration. He'd done it the right way, involving the town and allowing them to enjoy the party. He'd considered how he could help, not how he could tear down.

This party was his gift to the town...and she could tell from the gentle smile on his face, his gift to her as well.

Something of what she was feeling must have shown on her face because her mother laughed softly. "I told you that time would tell. You should go to him, haul him off to a nook or cranny, and let him know how you feel."

Chloe looked at her mother, uncertain what to do next. "But what if he doesn't feel the same way? I know he likes me. We've both admitted that several times, but what if he isn't falling in love with me the way I'm falling in love with him?"

"Then your heart will break," her mother murmured. "But it will have been worth it. Nothing is more important than love, and love is worth the risk. Go take it, daughter."

Chloe knew her mother was right. Love was worth the risk.

* * *

Evan looked at the two people who tugged him into the kitchen right when he'd been about to sweep Chloe into his arms and kiss her under the mistletoe.

Kitty and Dwayne Madison hadn't been home to Kringle since they'd moved their candy company to Dallas five years ago at Peter's behest.

But they were back now.

"I am so happy you've arranged all this, Mr. Conner," Kitty said for probably the tenth time since they'd arrived at the party.

Evan didn't mind her saying it again. Kitty and Dwayne were pleased with how everything was working out. "Please call me Evan," he invited. "I'm happy that you and Dwayne are happy. It's a good deal that works for everyone."

Dwayne nodded. "We were dying in Dallas. Lost in a sea of other candy companies. There was nothing special about us there. By moving, we lost what made us special. Kringle. People loved ordering from a candy company with the return address of Kringle, Texas. The town makes folks want to buy Christmas candy from us. Once we were in Dallas, no one cared."

Two days earlier, when Evan had called the Madisons to find out how things were going with their candy company, it didn't surprise him to discover how miserable they were.

They wanted to retire and return to Kringle, but their company, that had once done a booming business in Kringle, was dying on the vine in Dallas. The promises Peter had made them had never materialized. In fact, they'd laid off most of their employees because they were struggling.

But things were different now.

"Are you ready to go break the news to the rest of the town?" he asked, looking over his shoulder at the crowded family room behind him where people had been gathering to listen to the choir.

"We are." Mr. Madison nodded and took his wife's hand.

Evan signaled for the choir to stop after they finished their current song. Then he walked over to the normal-sized tree he'd had delivered and set up at the house the day before.

He lifted his arms. "Hello! Could I have your attention?"

The crowd quieted as every eye in the place fixed on him. Almost everyone was smiling at him, and he felt such a hit of pride that he'd put smiles on their faces. He scanned the group until he saw Chloe and smiled at her.

"We have an announcement to make." He motioned for Kitty and Dwayne to join him beside the tree. "I realize that introductions are unnecessary since most of you know Dwayne and Kitty."

A chorus of hellos and welcome backs emanated from the crowd.

"I've asked Dwayne and Kitty to join us tonight because we have some big news," Evan said, holding Chloe's gaze. "I've bought Kringle Kandy, and I plan to move it back to Kringle. I'm going to do a few updates and modifications, but based on my projections, and the contract commitments I've already secured, I expect the business to grow over the next few years."

People started cheering before he'd even stopped speaking. It took some time to get everyone settled down again, but eventually, he managed it. "I plan to stay on in Kringle and run the business," he told the crowd, grinning specifically at Chloe. "I've decided I like this place and the people who make Kringle what it is."

Another cheer went up through the group, and the crowd surged forward to shake his hand and clap him on the back. Evan wanted to break free and go find Chloe, but he knew that was going to take some time. He didn't want to be rude to these people. He liked and respected them.

But he couldn't help wishing a certain vet would come find him.

He had a few announcements to make to her as well.

* * *

Chloe felt desperate. She needed to talk to Evan —alone.

Townsfolk had overrun him after his announcement, and now she couldn't even see him. He was no longer in the family room. Where had he gone?

She walked through the house as quickly as possible, scanning each room for him. As more time passed, her anxiety grew.

Where was he? He couldn't have gone far.

She had to find him and tell him how she felt. Tell him that she was falling in love with him and find out if he felt the same way. Just knowing she might lose him made her heart ache. It was hard to believe that she could be falling in love with someone she'd only met a little over a week ago, but she was.

But how did he feel about her?

She just wasn't certain, and her knees were rubbery with fear. What if he didn't feel the same way?

When she finally found Evan, he was standing outside, looking up at the humongous tree. Chloe slipped out the back door and walked over to join him.

"Hey there," she murmured.

Evan didn't seem surprised to see her. He smiled. "Hey there, yourself."

She stepped closer to him, her heart thumping crazily.

Without saying another word, he gathered her close and kissed her.

She wrapped her arms around his neck and kissed him back. She poured all the love she felt for him into her kiss and hoped he could feel it too.

When they finally pulled apart, she smiled at him. "That was a friendly welcome. I've missed seeing you the last few days."

Evan hugged her closer. "I've missed you, too, but I needed to take care of a few things."

"I'll say." She gestured back at the house. "I hear Peter went back to Dallas," Chloe said, trying to work up the courage to say what she really wanted to say.

"Yes, he wasn't happy when I quit, so he decided he would have a better chance of having a perfect Christmas back in Dallas."

Chloe studied Evan. For a man who had just quit his job, bought a new company, and was upending his entire life, he seemed downright jovial. He had a wider smile on his handsome face than she'd ever seen.

"I'm glad you're happy," she whispered, leaning against him. "You really deserve it."

He gave her a gentle kiss. "Good. And I have exciting news."

"More exciting than this party?" she teased, bursting with love for this extraordinary man.

"Oh yes. Much more exciting."

A snowflake fell onto her face, followed by another and then another. "Look! It's snowing!"

They both looked up into the night sky. A flurry of flakes was now falling in the backyard.

"I knew it was cold out here, but I didn't think we'd have snow." She looked back up at the sky, quickly locating Orion's belt. "Look, you can see Orion very clearly tonight."

For a second, they looked at the sky speckled with stars and enjoyed the light snow falling on them. Chloe knew the smart move was to shift inside out of the snow, but the evening felt magical, and she wanted it to last as long as possible.

After a few moments, Evan asked, "How do you think Snowball will react to having Vixen around?"

When he brought up Snowball, she wasn't sure what he was getting at. "I think I need more information."

"I plan on adopting Vixen and her puppies. I love those dogs, so I'm going to make a home for them."

"All of them? Three puppies? That's quite a

commitment for someone who has never had a pet before. Puppies are a lot of work."

He flashed a wide grin. "I'm used to hard work, and I'm very dependable, so I know I'll make a good pet parent. I plan on naming them Dasher, Dancer, and Prancer," he said. "Dasher is the little one with the white dots because he looks like a runner. Dancer is the little brown one that likes to shimmy when happy. Finally, Prancer is the dark-brown one that is a real goofball."

It thrilled Chloe to hear that the dogs would all have a loving home, and she loved knowing he'd been noticing their personalities, but she had to ask, "You think you have room for all of them in your Dallas condo?"

Her question drew another smile from him. "I plan on buying this house. The Madisons say it's too big for them. They want a smaller place when they retire here, and I'm going to need a big house for all of my pets."

"Really? So you really are moving here?"

He flashed her a quick grin. "Yep. I want to stay," he said, kissing her lightly once again. "I'm sorry I didn't tell you about everything sooner, but I wanted to wait until I was sure the deal would go through. I had no idea what was going to happen, and then everything fell into place so quickly, I knew it was meant to be."

Chloe didn't mind a bit. "I understand. I'm just

overwhelmed. You plan to move here, but what about your career? What about corporate law?"

"I've spent the last few years helping other people create successful businesses. I think it's about time I created one for myself, and Kringle Kandy is the perfect business for me. The company really has so much potential."

The thought of running his own business excited him, and it thrilled her that he found something he'd enjoy.

Still, she couldn't shake the feeling that he was doing this just for her, so she asked, "Are you sure you are doing this for *you*? You didn't give up your job for me, did you? We can figure out some way to be together if you stay in Dallas, if that's what you really want. I don't want you to make a tremendous sacrifice to be with me."

A smile slowly grew on his face, and the twinkle in his eyes reassured her of his motivation. "I'm not making a sacrifice. I love Kringle."

Chloe couldn't believe how well everything was working out. She really was willing to move because she firmly believed that love was more important than where they lived, but now that would not be necessary.

The back door opened, and her mother appeared in the doorway. "Did you tell her yet?" she hollered.

Chloe glanced at the back of the house. People crowded against the windows, watching them.

"Um, what's going on?" she asked. "Everyone is looking at us."

Evan gave her a look filled with love. "They know I have something important to say to you."

Her heart pounded. "What's that?"

He drew her closer, looked down at her with wonder on his face. "Chloe Anderson, I love you."

Chloe felt tears well up in her eyes and run down her cheeks. She touched Evan's cheek. "Y-you love me?"

"I do. I love your laugh, and your upbeat attitude and the way you look in an elf costume. I know we've only known each other a short time, but I think we're working on something big and I hope you think so too."

"I do, I do!"

"There's no rush, we have all the time in the world, but maybe by next Christmas you'll say those words to me all over again."

Marriage to Evan? What a thrilling thought!

"I love you," she whispered so only he could hear it.

"I love you, too," he whispered back, and then he added, "Thank you so much for giving me the perfect Christmas gift of all."

"What gift is that?" she asked, a little confused. "I haven't given you your Christmas present yet."

"Oh, but you have." He smiled and kissed her

again. "You've given me the precious gift of your love."

And that's when Chloe knew that she had found the man she'd been waiting for.

* * *

Dear Reader,

Readers are an author's lifeblood, and the stories couldn't happen without you. Thank you so much for reading. If you enjoyed *A Perfect Christmas Gift,* I would so appreciate a review. You have no idea how much it means!

Please turn the page for an excerpt of the next book in the series, *A Perfect Christmas Wish* featuring Suzannah and Zach's romance.

If you'd like to keep up with my latest releases, you can sign up for my newsletter @ https://loriwilde.com/subscribe/

To check out my other books, you can visit me on the web @ www.loriwilde.com.

Much love and light!

—Lori

"You make a *terrible* Santa. You don't look a thing like him."

Zach Delaney glanced up and found Abby Owens, the ten-year-old daughter of his best friend, Suzannah, standing before him in the back room of Kringle Animal Clinic where he was getting dressed for the clinic's annual photo-with-Santa-for-pets day.

A frown marred her freckled face and preteen worry shimmered in her light blue eyes.

"I don't?" he asked, trying not to show his amusement. She looked so serious. "You sure?"

She nodded solemnly. As usual, Abby had an opinion. She was a confident, outspoken young lady, and Zach admired that about her. He was glad she wasn't afraid to express her opinions. Suzannah was doing an outstanding job of raising her after Keith had died.

"Not at all. You're a terrible Santa." Abby added a dramatic sigh and put a palm to her chest. "Terrible, terrible."

Zach glanced down at his costume. He was glad his appearance disappointed her. He didn't want to look like Santa. Heck, what healthy man in his thirties would?

"Thank you." He flashed her a smile. "I'm very glad to hear that."

"You shouldn't thank me." Abby tugged on the hem of his too-short sleeve, trying to pull it down over his wrist bones.

"Why not?" It was all he could do to keep the laughter from his voice. He didn't want Abby to think he was laughing at her. She *was* only ten. As much as she liked to consider herself an adult, she was still a child.

"You *should* worry. What if little kids see you? They'll be heartbroken that you aren't the real Santa. This is terrible."

"We can say I'm an amazingly good-looking Santa helper," he said. "Santa's helpers don't have to be perfect."

Abby released another dramatic sigh. "That won't work. This is awful. You need to look old, and you need a big belly."

"So, what are we going to do?" he asked.

"Hang on." She ran off, hollering, "Mom!"

Ah, reinforcement. Abby had gone to find the cavalry.

The holiday season was one of the many things Zach liked about his hometown of Kringle, Texas. Sure, Kringle had a bit of a holiday feeling about it year-round, but when December came, the town went into full-fledged Christmas mode.

Every street was decorated, and there was a constant stream of Christmas festivities. Even at the veterinarian clinic. It was impossible not to get caught up in the exuberant fun.

He would have preferred not to get caught up quite in this Christmas festivity. He wasn't a costume kind of guy.

While he waited for Abby to return, Zach considered the Santa costume the vet, Dr. Chloe Anderson, had given him to wear.

Suzannah worked for the Chloe as a receptionist,

and together, along with Abby, the two women had convinced him to dress as Santa for the annual Pet Pictures event.

He'd reluctantly agreed. Heck, he wouldn't have done it at all if Suzannah hadn't been the one asking, but he'd do just about anything for Suzannah and Abby. Even if it meant dressing up in a well-worn, extra-extra-large red velvet Santa costume.

Suzannah entered the backroom of the vet clinic trailed by her daughter who was gnawing on her bottom lip, twirling a strand of her long light brown hair around her index finger and shaking her head.

A smile curled Suzannah's lips. "I hear you don't have a belly like a bowl full of jelly."

"See, Mom? What did I tell you? *Ter-ri-ble.*"

Unlike Abby, Suzannah didn't seem the least bit bothered by his poorly fitting costume. Instead, she laughed. "Abby's right. You look awful in that outfit."

He couldn't say the same about her Mrs. Claus costume. As usual, it didn't matter what she wore, Suzannah was so beautiful it took his breath away.

She possessed pale blonde hair and deep blue eyes. The kind of eyes that reminded him of the Texas sky in summer.

Despite being a young, slim, vibrant woman, she'd done a good job of dressing up as a portly elderly lady. She had a tidy white wig on her head, little gold glasses perched on her nose, and plenty of padding all around.

"You look nice," he said.

"Nice?" She canted her head, that smile still lighting up her entire face, and rested her hands on her hips.

He chuckled. "Let me rephrase. You make a very attractive older woman," he added. "I can see why Santa married you."

She did a little twirl to show off her costume and batted her eyelashes. "I *am* quite the catch, aren't I?"

"Watch out. All the single men at the senior citizen will come a'courtin'," he teased.

She was a catch. He'd known it for decades, long before she married his best friend, Keith Owens. Long before Keith died in a motorcycle accident, leaving behind a heartbroken widow and a little daughter. Suzannah was special.

She seemed happy today. Over the course of the past three years, she and Abby had healed, but he knew she still missed Keith.

"So, what's the verdict? Can we save this mess?" he asked, sweeping a hand at his getup.

Having Suzannah hovering this close to him was difficult. More and more these days, he had trouble getting it through his thick cowboy skull that they were just friends. She smelled so good.

Like holiday cookies and spice cake. What they had felt like a heck of a lot more than just friendship. At least it did for him.

"You need more stuffing," she announced, stepping back and studying him again. "We need to make you look bigger. That'll help. Back in a jiff. Abs, come help me." She and Abby took off.

Zach sighed. Today definitely fit into the "no good deed goes unpunished" category. He'd agreed to help with these pictures, thinking it would be no big deal. How much did a guy have to look like Santa to pose with dogs and cats?

Apparently, quite a lot.

ABOUT THE AUTHOR

Lori Wilde is the New York Times, USA Today and Publishers' Weekly bestselling author of 87 works of romantic fiction. She's a three time Romance Writers' of America RITA finalist and has four times been nominated for Romantic Times Readers' Choice Award. She has won numerous other awards as well.

Her books have been translated into 26 languages, with more than four million copies of her books sold worldwide.

Her breakout novel, *The First Love Cookie Club*, has been optioned for a TV movie.

Lori is a registered nurse with a BSN from Texas Christian University. She holds a certificate in forensics, and is also a certified yoga instructor.

A fifth generation Texan, Lori lives with her husband, Bill, in the Cutting Horse Capital of the World; where they run Epiphany Orchards, a writing/creativity retreat for the care and enrichment of the artistic soul.

ALSO BY LORI WILDE

KRINGLE, TEXAS

A Perfect Christmas Gift

A Perfect Christmas Wish

A Perfect Christmas Surprise

A Perfect Christmas Joy

TEXAS RASCALS SERIES

Keegan

Matt

Nick

Kurt

Tucker

Kael

Truman

Dan

Rex

Clay

Jonah

Copyright © 2019 by Lori Wilde

All rights reserved.

No part of this book may be reproduced in any form or by any electronic or mechanical means, including information storage and retrieval systems, without written permission from the author, except for the use of brief quotations in a book review.